# TOEIC

## 練習測驗（6）

# LISTENING TEST

In the Listening test, you will be asked to demonstrate how well you understand spoken English. The entire Listening test will last approximately 45 minutes. There are four parts, and directions are given for each part. You must mark your answers on the separate answer sheet. Do not write your answers in your test book.

## PART 1

**Directions**: For each question in this part, you will hear four statements about a picture in your test book. When you hear the statements, you must select the one statement that best describes what you see in the picture. Then find the number of the question on your answer sheet and mark your answer. The statements will not be printed in your test book and will be spoken only one time.

Statement (C), "They're sitting at a table," is the best description of the picture, so you should select answer (C) and mark it on your answer sheet.

**1.**

**2.**

*GO ON TO THE NEXT PAGE.*

**3.**

**4.**

**5.**

**6.**

*GO ON TO THE NEXT PAGE.*

## PART 2

**Directions**: You will hear a question or statement and three responses spoken in English. They will not be printed in your test book and will be spoken only one time. Select the best response to the question or statement and mark the letter (A), (B), or (C) on your answer sheet.

7. Mark your answer on your answer sheet.

8. Mark your answer on your answer sheet.

9. Mark your answer on your answer sheet.

10. Mark your answer on your answer sheet.

11. Mark your answer on your answer sheet.

12. Mark your answer on your answer sheet.

13. Mark your answer on your answer sheet.

14. Mark your answer on your answer sheet.

15. Mark your answer on your answer sheet.

16. Mark your answer on your answer sheet.

17. Mark your answer on your answer sheet.

18. Mark your answer on your answer sheet.

19. Mark your answer on your answer sheet.

20. Mark your answer on your answer sheet.

21. Mark your answer on your answer sheet.

22. Mark your answer on your answer sheet.

23. Mark your answer on your answer sheet.

24. Mark your answer on your answer sheet.

25. Mark your answer on your answer sheet.

26. Mark your answer on your answer sheet.

27. Mark your answer on your answer sheet.

28. Mark your answer on your answer sheet.

29. Mark your answer on your answer sheet.

30. Mark your answer on your answer sheet.

31. Mark your answer on your answer sheet.

**Directions**: You will hear some conversations between two people. You will be asked to answer three questions about what the speakers say in each conversation. Select the best response to each question and mark the letter (A), (B), (C), or (D) on your answer sheet. The conversation will not be printed in your test book and will be spoken only one time.

**32.** What is the main topic of the conversation?
(A) A conference presentation.
(B) A building renovation.
(C) A reception for an executive.
(D) A budget review.

**33.** What does the man remind the woman to do?
(A) Arrive early at an event.
(B) Dress appropriately.
(C) Check an account.
(D) Reserve a table.

**34.** What will the woman be doing on Friday afternoon?
(A) Working outside of the office.
(B) Hosting an event.
(C) Interviewing a job applicant.
(D) Meeting a client.

**35.** What is the purpose of the call?
(A) To purchase some supplies.
(B) To return some merchandise.
(C) To make shipping arrangements.
(D) To locate a missing item.

**36.** What does the American man ask for?
(A) A tracking number.
(B) An inventory amount.
(C) The location of a building.
(D) The weight of package.

**37.** What does the woman say about the box?
(A) It is larger than average.
(B) It may have been damaged.
(C) It is needed soon.
(D) It is not brown.

**38.** What is the woman inquiring about?
(A) A payment option.
(B) A ticket upgrade.
(C) A flight schedule.
(D) A dinner reservation.

**39.** What does the woman say she needs to do at 5:00 p.m.?
(A) Give a presentation.
(B) Rent a hotel room.
(C) Meet some clients.
(D) Catch a connecting flight.

**40.** What does the man say he can do?
(A) Cancel a reservation.
(B) Take a later flight.
(C) Hold a table.
(D) Contact a client.

**41.** Where does the conversation take place?
(A) At a library.
(B) At a community center.
(C) At a concert hall.
(D) At an aquarium.

**42.** What additional membership benefit does the woman mention?
(A) Special classes.
(B) Gift certificates.
(C) Free parking.
(D) Discounted merchandise.

**43.** What does the woman ask the man to do?
(A) Present photo identification.
(B) Return at a later date.
(C) Complete some paperwork.
(D) Pick up a visitor's guide.

GO ON TO THE NEXT PAGE.

44. Where is the conversation most likely taking place?
   (A) At a restaurant.
   (B) At a butcher shop.
   (C) At a dry cleaners.
   (D) At a tourist center.

45. According to the woman, what is special about the product?
   (A) It is currently discounted.
   (B) It is only available today.
   (C) It is locally raised.
   (D) It is new this season.

46. What does the woman offer the man?
   (A) A business card.
   (B) An area map.
   (C) A handmade basket.
   (D) Free recipes.

47. Why is the man calling?
   (A) To recruit staff for an event.
   (B) To find a substitute for a night shift.
   (C) To ask for donations.
   (D) To cancel an advertisement.

48. What does the man mean when he says, "That's what I was afraid of"?
   (A) He expected the woman's response.
   (B) He didn't understand the woman's response.
   (C) He feared the woman's reaction.
   (D) He didn't appreciate the woman's reaction.

49. What will the man have to do?
   (A) Create a job description.
   (B) Reschedule a training session.
   (C) Try to find another volunteer.
   (D) Work the shift himself.

50. Why is the man calling?
   (A) To offer a new product.
   (B) To follow up on an estimate.
   (C) To inquire about a lease.
   (D) To arrange a maintenance visit.

51. What does the woman say she will be doing tomorrow?
   (A) Looking at apartments.
   (B) Attending a workshop.
   (C) Going on a trip.
   (D) Hosting a party.

52. What does the man ask the woman to do?
   (A) Make a deposit.
   (B) Complete a survey.
   (C) Move some furniture.
   (D) Leave a key at the front desk.

53. According to the woman, what is the company planning to do?
   (A) Merge with a media company.
   (B) Start an online magazine.
   (C) Relocate its headquarters.
   (D) Sponsor a local sports team.

54. What does the woman ask the man to do?
   (A) Meet with a client.
   (B) Lead a project.
   (C) Train some employees.
   (D) Write an article.

55. Why has the management chosen the man?
   (A) He is a professional cyclist.
   (B) He has lived abroad.
   (C) He has experience in Web site management.
   (D) He has organized many corporate events.

**56.** Why is the woman moving?
(A) Her lease has been expired.
(B) She is being transferred to a different city.
(C) There has been an increase in the rent.
(D) The apartment offers no parking.

**57.** What does the woman ask the man to do?
(A) Contact the moving company.
(B) Help her move out.
(C) Reduce a payment.
(D) Store some of her belongings.

**58.** What does the woman offer to do?
(A) Find a new tenant.
(B) Call the real estate agent.
(C) Write out a check.
(D) Sign the lease.

| Description | Unit Price | Total |
|---|---|---|
| FZR 9980 Silver 16GB GSM | $700.00 | $700.00 |
| Two-year Extended Warranty | $100.00 | $100.00 |
| Diamond Unlimited Service Plan (monthly) | $75.00 | $75.00 |
| Subtotal | | $875.00 |
| Sales Tax | | $76.56 |
| Shipping & Handling | | $0.00 |
| **Total Due** | | **$951.56** |

Due upon receipt

**Thank you for your business!**

**59.** What does the woman ask the man to do?
(A) Work overtime.
(B) Prepare an invoice.
(C) Schedule an appointment.
(D) Make a coworker's delivery.

**60.** What does the man say he needs?
(A) Keys to a vehicle.
(B) A telephone number.
(C) A price list.
(D) Directions to a location.

**61.** What does the woman remind the man to do?
(A) Print a document.
(B) Get a signature.
(C) Keep his receipts.
(D) Check some merchandise.

**62.** Who is the woman?
(A) A store clerk.
(B) A real estate agent.
(C) A banker.
(D) A teacher.

**63.** What does the man ask about?
(A) Additional features.
(B) Online payments.
(C) Trade-in policies.
(D) Coverage area.

**64.** Look at the graphic. Which charge will be removed from the bill?
(A) $75.00.
(B) $76.56.
(C) $100.
(D) $700.

*GO ON TO THE NEXT PAGE.*

**Admission Price per Person**

| | |
|---|---|
| University student | $18 |
| Group of 10 or more | $20 |
| Member | $15 |
| Nonmember | $25 |

---

| From: | Beau Tremonte <b.tremonte@cambercorp.com |
|---|---|
| To: | All Staff <all.list.staff@cambercorp.com |
| Re: | Sales Report |
| Date: | January 25 |

Hey folks, here's the updated schedule for the sales report meeting this afternoon. See you there!
  – Beau

2:00 p.m.  Eric Plonkenberg
                Sales Projection Assistance
3:00 p.m.  Vivian Wu
                Conference Agenda
**CANCELLED**  Joyce Figg
                Technology Seminar

---

**65.** What type of event are the speakers discussing?
(A) A theater performance.
(B) A museum exhibit opening.
(C) A photography workshop.
(D) A live music concert.

**66.** Look at the graphic. What ticket price will the speakers probably pay?
(A) $15.
(B) $18.
(C) $20.
(D) $25.

**67.** What does the woman suggest the man do?
(A) Pay with a credit card.
(B) Rent some equipment.
(C) Leave work early.
(D) Call a coworker.

**68.** Why is the man unable to access his e-mail?
(A) His password has expired.
(B) His Internet connection is not working.
(C) He forgot to update some software.
(D) He cancelled his Internet subscription.

**69.** Look at the graphic. Who sent the e-mail the speakers are referring to?
(A) Beau Tremonte.
(B) Eric Plonkenberg.
(C) Vivian Wu.
(D) Joyce Figg.

**70.** What does the man ask the woman to do?
(A) Print out a document.
(B) Review some sales figures.
(C) Inspect his computer.
(D) Prepare some training materials.

# PART 4

**Directions**: You will hear some talks given by a single speaker. You will be asked to answer three questions about what the speaker says in each talk. Select the best response to each question and mark the letter (A), (B), (C), or (D) on your answer sheet. The talks will not be printed in your test book and will be spoken only one time.

71. What item is being featured on the show?
    (A) A self-help book.
    (B) A plant container.
    (C) A set of gardening tools.
    (D) A portable generator.

72. What is Mr. Wise going to do?
    (A) Demonstrate the use of a product.
    (B) Answer questions from viewers.
    (C) Introduce the next guest.
    (D) Show a short video.

73. What is offered to the first 10 callers?
    (A) A ticket to the show.
    (B) Free shipping on an order.
    (C) A club membership.
    (D) A significant discount.

---

74. Where, most likely, does the speaker work?
    (A) At a convenience store.
    (B) At a talent agency.
    (C) At a brokerage firm.
    (D) At a cafe.

75. What is the problem?
    (A) Some items have not been delivered.
    (B) Some money is missing.
    (C) Some files have been misplaced.
    (D) Some customers are waiting.

76. What does the speaker mean by, "We're in big trouble"?
    (A) They will open an hour later.
    (B) They will fail an inspection.
    (C) They will be out of dairy products.
    (D) They will fire some employees.

77. What is the speaker about to do?
    (A) Issue identification cards.
    (B) Create work teams.
    (C) Talk about safety guidelines.
    (D) Inspect some equipment.

78. What are the listeners asked to provide?
    (A) An employee number.
    (B) A driver's license.
    (C) A personal reference.
    (D) An e-mail address.

79. What will happen at the end of the session?
    (A) A user's manual will be distributed.
    (B) Operators will use the new equipment.
    (C) A supervisor will hand out forms.
    (D) Participants will ask questions.

---

80. What has the listener agreed to do?
    (A) Prepare some training materials.
    (B) Deliver some packages.
    (C) Speak at an event.
    (D) Help plan a conference.

81. What did the speaker send in an e-mail?
    (A) A registration form.
    (B) A tentative itinerary.
    (C) A list of hotels.
    (D) A flight schedule.

82. What is the speaker specifically interested in?
    (A) Price per room.
    (B) Transportation.
    (C) Internet access.
    (D) Meeting facilities.

*GO ON TO THE NEXT PAGE.*

83. What kind of business does the speaker work in?
- (A) Banking.
- (B) Travel.
- (C) Retail sales.
- (D) Auto insurance.

84. According to the speaker, what advantage does the new location have?
- (A) It has more parking spaces.
- (B) It uses green technology.
- (C) It is easily accessible by public transportation.
- (D) It is close to a variety of restaurants.

85. What policy change does the speaker mention?
- (A) Weekly meetings will be optional.
- (B) Travel expenses will be reimbursed.
- (C) Employees will have more vacation time.
- (D) Telecommuting options will be offered.

86. What is the main purpose of the message?
- (A) To announce a closing.
- (B) To request a deadline extension.
- (C) To report a network issue.
- (D) To explain a firing decision.

87. What is expected to happen by the evening?
- (A) New security measures will go into effect.
- (B) Weather conditions will be severe.
- (C) Power will be restored.
- (D) Construction will begin.

88. What are listeners reminded to do?
- (A) Update a schedule.
- (B) Locate a contractor.
- (C) Report damage to a supervisor.
- (D) Turn off some equipment.

89. Who are the listeners?
- (A) Engineers.
- (B) Beauticians.
- (C) Board members.
- (D) News reporters.

90. What does the speaker mean when he says "Adding insult to injury"?
- (A) To emphasize the point.
- (B) To lessen our burden.
- (C) To make a long story short.
- (D) To make things worse.

91. What does the speaker propose?
- (A) Launching an advertising campaign.
- (B) Lodging a formal complaint.
- (C) Renovating a facility.
- (D) Merging with a competitor.

| Tiger Mart Anniversary Two-for-One Blow Out Sale! | |
| --- | --- |
| **Sales Item** | **Store Location** |
| Storage Boxes | Woodridge |
| Water purification filters | Willowbrook |
| Car wax and polish | Downers Grove |
| Desk lamps | Burr Ridge |

92. Look at the graphic. At which store location is the announcement being made?
- (A) Hinsdale.
- (B) Downers Grove.
- (C) Woodridge.
- (D) Burr Ridge.

93. What is Tiger Mart celebrating?
- (A) A national holiday.
- (B) A profitable quarter.
- (C) An anniversary.
- (D) A new store opening.

94. Why should listeners visit a Web site?
- (A) To check for coupons.
- (B) To write a customer review.
- (C) To vote for the employee of the week.
- (D) To sign up for a rewards program.

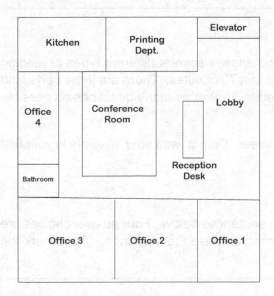

| | | | Elevator |
|---|---|---|---|
| Kitchen | Printing Dept. | | |
| Office 4 | Conference Room | Lobby | |
| Bathroom | | Reception Desk | |
| Office 3 | Office 2 | Office 1 | |

**CROSS-TRAINING SCHEDULE**

**Department / Date**

**Personnel /**
**Monday (a.m.) – Tuesday (a.m.)**

**Purchasing /**
**Monday (p.m.) – Tuesday (p.m.)**

**Warehouse / Wednesday**

**Technical support /**
**Thursday (a.m.) – Friday (a.m.)**

**Marketing /**
**Thursday (p.m.) – Friday (p.m.)**

95. What type of report is the speaker requesting?
(A) Office inventory.
(B) Employee evaluations.
(C) Expense reports.
(D) Travel receipts.

96. Look at the graphic. Which office belongs to the speaker?
(A) Office 1.
(B) Office 2.
(C) Office 3.
(D) Office 4.

97. Why does the speaker postpone a deadline?
(A) She wants a job to be done thoroughly.
(B) She needs to interview more people.
(C) She knows the listener is busy.
(D) She will not be able to review some documents until later.

98. When is this talk most likely taking place?
(A) On Monday.
(B) On Tuesday.
(C) On Thursday.
(D) On Friday.

99. Look at the graphic. Which department will listeners visit on Friday afternoon?
(A) Technical support.
(B) Purchasing.
(C) Marketing.
(D) Personnel.

100. What will happen after the morning session?
(A) Instructors will give a demonstration.
(B) A meeting will be held.
(C) Identification cards will be distributed.
(D) Lunch will be provided.

This is the end of the Listening test. Turn to Part 5 in your test book.

GO ON TO THE NEXT PAGE.

# READING TEST

In the Reading test, you will read a variety of texts and answer several different types of reading comprehension questions. The entire Reading test will last 75 minutes. There are three parts, and directions are given for each part. You are encouraged to answer as many questions as possible within the time allowed.

You must mark your answers on the separate answer sheet. Do not write your answers in your test book.

## PART 5

**Directions**: A word or phrase is missing in each of the sentences below. Four answer choices are given below each sentence. Select the best answer to complete the sentence. Then mark the letter (A), (B), (C), or (D) on your answer sheet.

**101.** Mr. Wang had hoped that the new office would be ------- to the subway station.
(A) closely
(B) closest
(C) closing
(D) closer

**102.** The Viewer Tool offers a wide range of solutions ------- viewing the contents of damaged files of various formats.
(A) as
(B) in
(C) for
(D) with

**103.** T.E.K. Consulting is well known for its training program, ------- allows employees to switch places with one of their peers.
(A) which
(B) whose
(C) it
(D) itself

**104.** To comply with our policy, customers must present a valid sales receipt when returning any -------.
(A) ticket
(B) survey
(C) feature
(D) merchandise

**105.** The mechanic could not repair the car because he did not have the right -------.
(A) equip
(B) equipping
(C) equipped
(D) equipment

**106.** The ------- installed software will decrease the amount of time it takes to pack and ship orders.
(A) fast
(B) very
(C) soon
(D) recently

**107.** Parking fees are charged on weekdays, with ------- permit and metered spaces available.
(A) while
(B) both
(C) once
(D) there

**108.** We will ------- the tasks related to the marketing campaign evenly among all staff members.
(A) sample
(B) suggest
(C) split
(D) suspend

**109.** To reduce glare in the summer months, the building was equipped with the ------- windows available.
(A) darker
(B) darkest
(C) darkly
(D) darkness

**110.** Most survey participants responded that they ------- watched news programming on Saturday evenings.
(A) alike
(B) instead
(C) rather
(D) seldom

**111.** ------- of the apartments has its own private entrance.
(A) Such
(B) All
(C) Each
(D) Everyone

**112.** Business casual attire is considered ------- for the Megatrends Marketing Seminar.
(A) significant
(B) appropriate
(C) useful
(D) complete

**113.** A new terminal is expected to open at the airport next month, and it ------- for an increase in the number of passengers.
(A) allow
(B) will allow
(C) allowed
(D) has allowed

**114.** Jefferson Industries is seeking employees with an excellent ------- of both written and spoken Spanish.
(A) excess
(B) description
(C) command
(D) belief

**115.** The film was received ------- well at the box-office and was one of the biggest hits of the year.
(A) exceptionally
(B) exceptional
(C) except
(D) exception

**116.** Mr. Brown pays ------- attention to the expense accounts and travel itineraries of the sales team.
(A) particular
(B) substantial
(C) granted
(D) provided

**117.** ------- pizza boxes are often soaked with grease, they are often not accepted by municipal recycling programs.
(A) Just
(B) Even
(C) Because
(D) In fact

**118.** Using the latest technology, we're able to offer our customers a wide ------- of printing options to suit their needs.
(A) variety
(C) way
(B) kind
(D) deposit

**119.** Employees must be aware that their Internet ------- will be closely monitored.
(A) used
(B) uses
(C) usage
(D) using

**120.** It would be four to six weeks before they would know ------- the marketing campaign was successful.
(A) until
(B) so that
(C) whether
(D) as

*GO ON TO THE NEXT PAGE.*

**121.** The goal was ------- more data, from a wider variety of sources, in a shorter amount of time.
(A) analysis
(B) analyze
(C) analyzed
(D) to analyze

**122.** Each of us took turns thanking Mr. Combs personally on the phone -------- he insisted it was unnecessary.
(A) as if
(B) although
(C) but
(D) nevertheless

**123.** Despite the multiple uses of the product, it failed ------- enthusiasm amongst consumers.
(A) generated
(B) generating
(C) will generate
(D) to generate

**124.** The donation will go ------- construction of the business school's new site in the Manhattanville section of New York City.
(A) toward
(B) past
(C) near
(D) within

**125.** The pharmaceutical industry is a highly competitive business and its success is ------- on the marketing and sales of each drug.
(A) dependable
(B) dependent
(C) depend
(D) depends

**126.** To prevent milk and other ------- products from deteriorating, ABCO's goods are stored in a cold warehouse.
(A) constructive
(B) adverse
(C) plentiful
(D) perishable

**127.** Heartland Foods purchased 120 stores from ------- distressed owners.
(A) financing
(B) financial
(C) financially
(D) financed

**128.** The new monitoring technology empowers people to make continued and ------- improvements to their energy efficiency.
(A) measurable
(B) vague
(C) severe
(D) prompt

**129.** After ------- with local residents, construction of a new library was suspended indefinitely.
(A) deliberate
(B) deliberation
(C) deliberately
(D) deliberated

**130.** Restaurateurs have been permitted in some jurisdictions to build ------- smoking areas separate from dining areas.
(A) fashioned
(B) featured
(C) differentiated
(D) designated

**Directions**: Read the texts that follow. A word or phrase is missing in some of the sentences. Four answer choices are given below each of the sentences. Select the best answer to complete the text. Then mark the letter (A), (B), (C), or (D) on your answer sheet.

**Questions 131-134** refer to the following e-mail.

| |
|---|
| From: Trask Home Station <info@traskhome.com> |
| To: Stephan Chicco <c_chicco@intermail.com> |

Dear Mr. Chicco,

Thank you for purchasing your new Sontron dishwasher from Trask Home Station. The ------- is scheduled to be delivered to 624 Green
    **131.**
Road on November 5 between 1:00 p.m. and 5:00 p.m.

-------. The delivery personnel will unload, uncrate and place the
**132.**

appliance in the requested room setting.

Your invoice will be sent electronically on the same day.

Please be reminded that we charge $150.00 for orders canceled within
24 hours of delivery or if ------- is at home to accept the delivery.
    **133.**

Please give us a call ------- you have any questions.
    **134.**

**131.** (A) segment
(B) addition
(C) item
(D) detail

**132.** (A) Delivery will be made by a two-man team trained to install and set up your dishwasher
(B) Appointments will be scheduled three weeks in advance of your session
(C) These hours are similar to those of other restaurants
(D) Customers have already posted some online reviews

**133.** (A) no one
(B) nothing
(C) neither
(D) not

**134.** (A) so
(B) that
(C) if
(D) or

GO ON TO THE NEXT PAGE.

Global Commerce Insider (GCI) ------- authoritative insight
135.

and opinion on international news for 25 years.  With its

reputation for thorough analysis of world business and

current affairs, GCI is ------- reading for business leaders as
136.

well as future market leaders.

-------.
137.

To obtain a free trial -------, call (800)-599-5677.
138.

**135.** (A) have been provided
(B) had provided
(C) will provide
(D) has been providing

**136.** (A) requirements
(B) required
(C) require
(D) requirement

**137.** (A) A ten-year service agreement includes free oil changes and filters on a monthly basis as directed by your service plan
(B) A two-fold increase of online membership applications is expected to overwhelm our servers
(C) A one-month deposit is required upon signing of the lease, which will be refunded when the lease expires
(D) A one-year subscription comes with online access to world stock market reports updated daily at www.gci.com.

**138.** (A) standard
(B) right
(C) issue
(D) entry

Dear Ms. Larsen,

As we discussed on the phone last week, we are going to meet on May 31 and June 6. We are going to evaluate the T-Star videoconferencing system. It is very important to find out whether the system has been ------- in general. If
**139.**

necessary, we can adjust the system to suit your needs.

-------, options for adding contacts and managing group
**140.**

sessions can be modified. The meeting ------- at 2:00 p.m.
**141.**

in your office. -------. I look forward to seeing you on
**142.**

March 28.

**139.** (A) effectiveness
(B) effect
(C) effectively
(D) effective

**140.** (A) Rather
(B) Even so
(C) For instance
(D) Unless

**141.** (A) were held
(B) have been held
(C) to hold
(D) will be held

**142.** (A) Should there be a delay, don't hesitate to cancel your appointment
(B) If you have any questions or concerns, please feel free to call me
(C) You can take the shuttle from the airport to the hotel
(D) Most orders are shipped within 5-7 business days

*GO ON TO THE NEXT PAGE.*

Nirvana Sound and Vision is the most trusted name in professional audio sales in southwest Oregon. ------- its **143.** president Matthew Sands, founded Nirvana Sound and Vision 10 years ago, the company has established great customer service. -------. According to Mr. Sands, he ------- **144.** **145.** this recognition by offering personal attention to customers. Mr. Sands believes that a focus on treating customers like family has helped the business develop a solid ------- for outstanding quality and reliability. **146.**

**143.** (A) When
(B) Until
(C) While
(D) Since

**144.** (A) Consequently, Nirvana closed most of its operations in Oregon
(B) Meanwhile, digital audio sales continue to decline
(C) Additionally, the company will offer wedding packages beginning in March
(D) In fact, it was rated as the number one audio/video retailer in southwest Oregon this year

**145.** (A) was earning
(B) will earn
(C) will be earned
(D) has earned

**146.** (A) compliment
(B) acquaintance
(C) reputation
(D) familiarity

**Directions**: In this part you will read a selection of texts, such as magazine and newspaper articles, e-mails, and instant messages. Each text or set of texts is followed by several questions. Select the best answer for each question and mark the letter (A), (B), (C), or (D) on your answer sheet.

**Questions 147-148** refer to the following notice.

## ATTENTION CHAPEL HILL HOMEOWNERS

In an effort to reduce our carbon footprint, the Chapel Hill Homeowner's Association (CHHA) is moving online and going paperless. As of September 1, all association-related communications, our monthly newsletter, resident directory, and advisory notifications will be issued via our Web site, at www.chha.org.

Please visit our Web site at your earliest convenience to sign up for our automated e-mail alert system, which will keep you up-to-date with CHHA activities and announcements. Meanwhile, please look over the resident directory to confirm that your information is accurate. Feel free to call me with corrections.

Thanks,

Randall Emerson
Chapel Hill Homeowner's Association
384-0099

147. What change will be made to the monthly newsletter?
(A) It will be edited by a homeowner.
(B) It will cover more than one neighborhood.
(C) It will include advertisements.
(D) It will be available only online.

148. According to the notice, why might readers contact Mr. Emerson?
(A) To subscribe to a newsletter.
(B) To suggest changes in deadlines.
(C) To request a correction.
(D) To list a property for sale.

*GO ON TO THE NEXT PAGE.*

# JC Electronics

## Our Return Policy

- Non-defective products must be returned within thirty days (30) from the date of purchase, unless otherwise indicated.

- Returned product must be in original packaging, unused, undamaged and in saleable condition.

- Proof of purchase is required and all non-warranted items are subject to a 15% restocking fee.

149. What is the purpose of the notice?
(A) To announce an event.
(B) To explain a policy.
(C) To advertise a product.
(D) To recruit new employees.

150. What is stated about items to be returned?
(A) A manager must approve the transaction.
(B) The price tag must be attached to them.
(C) They are accepted for a limited period of time.
(D) They must be sent back to the manufacturer.

LINK UP Co-working Office: Connect, Network, Inspire

Thank you for your interest in LINK UP. Please complete the request form below. We will contact you shortly with the plan and pricing that will suit the needs of your group.

Name: _____

Contact Number: _____

E-mail: _____     Phone: _____

Date(s): _____

Location preference:
[ ] LINK UP Cedar Rapids     [ ] LINK UP Des Moines
[ ] LINK UP Davenport

Membership Plan
[ ] Drop-in/Daily Pass     [ ] Full-time     [ ] Non-profit
[ ] Corporate (name of organization): _____

Number of memberships: [ ] Single     [ ] 2-5     [ ] 6+

Business center access required: [ ] Yes     [ ] No
Computer rental: [ ] Yes     [ ] No

LINK UP Co-working Space: Connect, Network, Inspire

**151.** According to the form, what will Crossroads LINK UP staff do?
(A) Calculate a rate based on the information submitted.
(B) Reserve a conference room.
(C) Provide discounts for more than six memberships.
(D) Assist participants on the day of an event.

**152.** What is true about LINK UP?
(A) It recently began operating its own non-profit organization.
(B) It requires members to log into a Web site.
(C) It is not accepting new members.
(D) It has three locations.

GO ON TO THE NEXT PAGE.

Bright Eyes Vision Clinic
98 East 12th Avenue
New York, NY 10012

April 10

Ethan Feldman
248 Astoria Avenue
Queens, NY 11009

Dear Mr. Feldman:

At Bright Eyes Vision Clinic, the doctors and our entire optometry team are committed to providing advanced vision care in a professional and comfortable environment. Therefore, it is essential that your account information be up-to-date. Effective May 1, all invoices are due within 30 days of service. Please find enclosed a complete and detailed explanation of our revised billing schedule.

The revision allows us to continue to provide clinical care to you and your family without increasing the cost of services this year. Should you need to make alternate payment arrangements, please contact our office manager, George McMahon, at (212)909-1212.

Sincerely,
Bright Eyes Vision Clinic

**153.** Why was the letter sent to Mr. Feldman?
(A) To attract new patients.
(B) To announce a policy change.
(C) To reschedule an appointment.
(D) To promote a newly upgraded clinic.

**154.** What is indicated about Bright Eyes Vision Clinic?
(A) It caters to low-income patients.
(B) It has updated its hours of operation.
(C) It has hired a new office manager.
(D) It hopes to avoid an increase in fees.

Carlos Betancourt, Recollections, 2010, C-print mounted on Plexiglas, © Carlos Betancourt

The first piece from Carlos Betancourt's "Baroque to Bling" series has gained international recognition following exhibitions in museums and galleries around the world, including the Art Institute of Chicago, the Warhol Gallery in Pittsburgh, and the Louvre in Paris. *Recollections* was featured on the cover of The Atlantic Monthly in September of last year. Originally purchased by Donna McMillan for her private collection, the piece was donated to the Palm Springs Art Museum for our permanent collection last month. The Baroque to Bling works offer contemporary interpretations of the baroque, a term that brings to mind lavishly ornamental design, elaborate aesthetics, and a sense of the theatrical.

**155.** Where is the information posted?
(A) At the Louvre.
(B) At the Warhol Gallery.
(C) At the Art Institute of Chicago.
(D) At the Palm Springs Art Museum.

**156.** Who, most likely, is Ms. McMillan?
(A) A sculptor.
(B) An art historian.
(C) An art collector.
(D) A gallery manager.

**157.** What is NOT stated about Recollections?
(A) It belongs to a series of works.
(B) It has had more than one owner.
(C) It appeared on the cover of The Atlantic Monthly.
(D) The artist considers it to be one of his best works.

GO ON TO THE NEXT PAGE.

Steam Pressure Washer – Grime Fighter- $500 (Cupertino)

Posting Description:

I haven't used this washer in a while; the gun and hoses are missing. Will also need a fuel pump ($50). The unit worked great last year when we used it on the tractor, but the fuel pump has since corroded.

This machine would be well over a thousand if it were in top condition, but since it needs that fuel pump, gun, and hoses, I'm asking $500 or best offer. Welcome to come check it out anytime. As you can see in the pics, it's been kept clean.

Reply to: call or text me for address: 673-5566

**158.** What is NOT indicated about the pressure washer?
(A) It has had more than one owner.
(B) It has been kept clean.
(C) It needs a new fuel pump.
(D) Its hasn't been used in a while.

**159.** What is the seller willing to do?
(A) Ship the item to a buyer.
(B) Negotiate a price.
(C) Include an extra fuel pump.
(D) Extend the warranty.

**160.** What is implied about the ad?
(A) It includes photographs.
(B) It was posted in a newspaper.
(C) It was posted several weeks earlier.
(D) It only applies to residents of Cupertino.

---

## TREVOR YOUNT: Executive V.P., Global Human Resources

As Eclipse's Chief Human Resource Officer, Trevor's responsibilities include talent scouting, development, inspiration, retention and infrastructure planning for all worldwide employees in the Eclipse brand and affiliate organizations (Runverse Inc. and Turley International LLC). Prior to Eclipse, Trevor led the Talent and Performance Division at SaberCo. In this role, he was responsible for compensation and benefits policy setting, plan design and administration for 160,000 employees worldwide and for the company's talent management functions. During his career at SaberCo he held a variety of international positions that included eight years based in international markets. Prior to joining SaberCo, Trevor led the human resources division for Filmore and Pierce Management Consultants. Trevor holds degrees from two Ivy League universities ——an economics and accounting degree from Dartmouth College and an MBA in finance from Harvard. He has more than 20 years of human resource corporate and consulting experience.

---

161. What is the purpose of the information?
    (A) To detail an executive's nomination for an award.
    (B) To announce the winner of a competition.
    (C) To profile a company employee.
    (D) To summarize an employee's current research.

162. What is NOT indicated as one of Mr. Yount's current responsibilities?
    (A) Talent scouting.
    (B) Product marketing.
    (C) Infrastructure planning.
    (D) Employee retention.

163. What is suggested about Mr. Yount?
    (A) He attended college in Canada.
    (B) He was an accountant at SaberCo.
    (C) His responsibilities are very broad.
    (D) His career is almost over.

GO ON TO THE NEXT PAGE.

| From: | Mike <m_cleary@currentmail.com> |
|---|---|
| To: | Kendra <k_fulton@currentmail.com> |
| Re: | Schedule Update |
| Date: | May 23 |

Kendra:

Just one quick change to your schedule tomorrow. Your client Lou Pristo called this evening and requested to reschedule your meeting for later in the afternoon tomorrow. Since you're leaving for the conference at 3:30, I suggested we move it back to next Thursday, which is May 31. Do you want to confirm this appointment? Also, you'll see that I've filled Mr. Pristo's time slot with the pending review of the factory prototypes. Let me know if that doesn't work for you.

| Time | Appointment | Attendees |
|---|---|---|
| 7:45 a.m. | Breakfast @ Over Easy Café | Richard Loeb<br>Mai Truong |
| 9:00 a.m. | Team meeting: Midwest Sales Conference | Lee Vanderburg<br>Dina Saedi |
| 11:00 a.m. | Review of factory prototypes | Cole Zendik |
| Noon | Lunch @ Kingsbury | John Platt<br>Dina Saedi |
| 1:45 p.m. | Marketing meeting | Julie Jones |
| 3:30 p.m. | Car service to Lambert-St. Louis Int'l Airport | |

Meanwhile, printed copies of your hotel and flight confirmation are on your desk, so you'll see them first thing when you come in tomorrow.

Cheers,
Mike

**164.** Why was the e-mail sent?
   (A) To discuss an agenda for a meeting.
   (B) To provide a revised daily schedule.
   (C) To change a travel itinerary.
   (D) To confirm a restaurant reservation.

**165.** What will most likely happen on May 31?
   (A) Ms. Saedi will give a presentation at a conference.
   (B) Mr. Spence will purchase a train ticket.
   (C) Mr. Pristo will meet with Ms. Fulton.
   (D) Ms. Moore will return from St. Louis.

**166.** Which of the following is something Mike Spence has done for Kendra Fulton?
   (A) Cancelled an appointment.
   (B) Printed some documents.
   (C) Opened her mail.
   (D) Paid for a meal.

**167.** At what time was Mr. Pristo expected?
   (A) 7:45 a.m.
   (B) 9:00 a.m.
   (C) 11:00 a.m.
   (D) 3:30 p.m.

GO ON TO THE NEXT PAGE.

Orion Bicycles

Progress Report for the week of November 8-12
Carla Roberts, Project Lead

This week's progress:

Researched several manufacturing companies in Guadalajara, Mexico, with experience making custom bicycle seats. ---[1]--- Sent schematics of our new seat design and inquired about logistics: minimum order quantity, shipping, production, and turnaround time, ETC. ---[2]---

Based on initial discussions, Avendia Industrias seems to be the manufacturer that will work for us. ---[3]---. Likewise, Juan Garza, the factory sales manager got back to me right away with a detailed quote. He seemed very accommodating and eager for our business. My intuition tells me we'd have a solid business relationship with Avendia.

Contacted four other companies that were either out of our price range or unable to accommodate our schedule. ---[4]---. Thus, no longer in contention for our business.

Plans for the week of November 15-19

Continue discussions with Avendia Industrias about project needs and invoicing terms.
Have the design team outline the steps of the production process. Submit this information to Avendia so that a prototype can be manufactured.

**168.** What is suggested about Orion Bicycles?

(A) It is relocating to Mexico.

(B) It is hiring a sales manager.

(C) It is developing a new product.

(D) It is closing a facility.

**169.** According to the report, what did Ms. Roberts do during the week of November 8?

(A) She finalized shipping schedules.

(B) She acquired new machinery.

(C) She interviewed potential factory employees.

(D) She evaluated possible business partners.

**170.** What is mentioned about Mr. Garza?

(A) He will travel to meet Ms. Roberts in person.

(B) He is part of the design team.

(C) He asked few questions.

(D) He is very accommodating.

**171.** In which of the positions marked [1], [2], [3], and [4] does the following sentences best belong?

"They are a relatively new and smaller company, but are willing to hire additional staff to complete our order."

(A) [1].

(B) [2].

(C) [3].

(D) [4].

*GO ON TO THE NEXT PAGE.*

Regine Nilo [3:02 p.m.]  Tony, something is wrong with the shopping cart on our Web site.  It doesn't open when you click on the icon; a customer just called to complain that she can't process her transaction.

Anthony Swift [3:03 p.m.]  Uh-oh.  When did the problem start?

Regine Nilo [3:04 p.m.]  **No clue.**  I was alerted by the customer.  It's the first I'm hearing about it.  Can you get in touch with someone from IT and find out what's going on?

Anthony Swift [3:05 p.m.]  Doug, the shopping cart function is down on the Web site.  Do you have any idea what's happening?

Doug Rapier [3:06 p.m.]  Yeah, one of my programmers entered a line of bad code during routine maintenance.  We're looking for it right now.

Anthony Swift [3:09 p.m.]  I hope you can get it back up and running soon.

Doug Rapier [3:16 p.m.]  Depends, but probably not longer than an hour.  I've got the whole team on it.

Anthony Swift [3:21 p.m.]  The sooner the better, Doug.  By the way, let Regine know when you fix it.  I'll need her to write some kind of apology and notification for the landing page.

Regine Nilo [3:22 p.m.]  I'm already on it, Tony.  Doug, I just emailed you a draft.  Can you put it in a small, tasteful banner?

Doug Rapier [3:26 p.m.]  Got it.  Consider it done.  Sorry about the issue, guys.  We just found the error, and it should be resolved in the next minute or two when the system is refreshed.

**172.** What problem does Ms. Nilo report?
  (A) The company's Web site cannot be accessed.
  (B) Some product information is incorrect.
  (C) Payments cannot be processed in the online store.
  (D) The company's Web site is re-directing customers to another site.

**173.** From whom did Ms. Nilo learn about the problem?
  (A) A consultant.
  (B) A supervisor.
  (C) A customer.
  (D) An IT coworker.

**174.** What does Mr. Rapier say caused the problem?
  (A) Human error.
  (B) Too much Internet traffic.
  (C) A new program.
  (D) A technical issue with their service provider.

**175.** At 3:04, what does Ms. Nilo most likely mean when she writes, "No clue."
  (A) She is concerned about the sales report.
  (B) She has already spoken to somebody in IT.
  (C) She has never used the shopping cart function.
  (D) She doesn't know when the problem began.

*GO ON TO THE NEXT PAGE.*

| From: | g.sterling@panorama.com |
|-------|-------------------------|
| To: | d.bernardo@shuttershow.net |
| Re: | Panorama's Photography Digest |
| Date: | August 11 |

Dear Mr. Bernardo,

Panorama's Photography Digest is offering discounted advertising rates to first-time advertisers.  For a limited time, when you place an ad in Panorama's Photography Digest, you can reach a targeted audience of over 60,000 photography professionals in print and online.  Expand your customer base by taking advantage of this unique opportunity.

Outlined below are our current offers for first-time advertisers, valid until September 15.  To reserve any of these full-color advertisements, have one of our designers create a custom layout for you, or request more information, please reply to this e-mail or call me at 404-800-0103 ext. 33.  Specifications for advertisements are available at www.panorama.com/ads.

Sincerely,
Gwen Sterling
Marketing Coordinator
Panorama's Photography Digest

| From: | d.bernardo@shuttershow.net |
|---|---|
| To: | g.sterling@panorama.com |
| Re: | Panorama's Photography Digest |
| Date: | August 12 |

Hello Ms. Sterling,

I received your e-mail and am interested in placing an advertisement in Panorama's Photography Digest. However, I need some clarification about the online advertisement. The specifications on your Web site are unclear about the location of the advertisement. Where exactly would the 4"x5" advertisement appear on your Web site?

Please get back to me at your earliest convenience, and I can provide an electronic file of the advertisement together with my credit card information.

Thanks,

Doug Bernardo
Owner

**176.** Why did Ms. Sterling e-mail Mr. Bernardo?
(A) To inform him of a special promotion.
(B) To offer him a discount on a subscription.
(C) To announce the launch of a publication.
(D) To advertise a new agricultural product.

**177.** What is suggested about Panorama's Photography Digest?
(A) It publishes a full-color magazine.
(B) It recently expanded its readership.
(C) It will be releasing a special issue.
(D) It has increased its advertising rates.

**178.** What is implied about Mr. Bernardo?
(A) He has never advertised with Panorama.
(B) He will be out of the office in October.
(C) He is a graphic designer.
(D) He has worked with Ms. Sterling before.

**179.** In the second e-mail, the word "unclear" in paragraph 1, line 3, is closest in meaning to
(A) on hold.
(B) in doubt.
(C) at once.
(D) for certain.

**180.** What concern does Mr. Bernardo have?
(A) Deadline for the next issue.
(B) Placement of the advertisement.
(C) Appropriate digital file type.
(D) Size of the page.

*GO ON TO THE NEXT PAGE*

| From: | t.chou@thompsondigital.com |
|---|---|
| To: | r.harvey@bullseye.net |
| Re: | Thompson Digital Marketing – Graphic Design |
| Date: | Wednesday, June 9 |

Dear Ms. Harvey,

We enjoyed meeting you during our interview on Monday and believe you will be a tremendous asset to the graphic design team at Thompson Digital Marketing. You will provide creative support in the creation and analysis of marketing and communication deliverables including, but not limited to brochures, direct mail pieces, onsite collateral, signs and banners, website graphics, print ads, social media, e-mail campaigns, and other visuals. You will execute and maintain high quality sales collateral based on direction and branding of the company.

Your assignment will commence in July with a two-day training session at our headquarters in Palo Alto, California. We're hoping to select a time that's convenient for as many people on the new team as possible, especially those like you who will be moving from out-of-state. Please respond to this e-mail as soon as possible and let me know what starting date in July you prefer.

This is a contract position, and aside from the initial training session, work will be done remotely, meaning you are free to set your own hours and schedule. As discussed, design projects are compensated at a variable rate depending on the complexity of the assignment. Marsalis Tull, our head of human resources, will be in touch soon with all the necessary documents you will need to fill out.

We look forward to working with you!

Tiffany Chou
Thompson Digital Marketing

| From: | t.chou@thompsondigital.com |
|---|---|
| To: | All Graphic Designers |
| Re: | Thompson Digital Marketing – Graphic Design |
| Date: | June 9 |

Dear Graphic Design Team,

Based on your feedback, it appears that July 16-17 works best for most of you. Please note that training will run from Saturday morning through Sunday afternoon. We expect anyone who lives outside the area to arrive on Thursday, July 14, when we will arrange for you to have dinner with some of our local designers if you like. All travel expenses will be covered by Thompson Digital Marketing. More details about this will follow, but for now I just want to inform you of the schedule so you can put it on your calendars.

Tiffany Chou
Thompson Digital Marketing

**181.** Why did Ms. Chou write to Ms. Harvey?
(A) To promote a writing workshop.
(B) To negotiate a salary.
(C) To offer her a position.
(D) To provide technical assistance.

**182.** What information is Ms. Harvey asked to provide?
(A) A list of her current clients.
(B) Her educational background.
(C) Her availability for training.
(D) A summary of her work experience.

**183.** Why will Mr. Tull contact Ms. Harvey?
(A) To issue employment paperwork.
(B) To explain software requirements.
(C) To clarify a company policy.
(D) To make travel arrangements.

**184.** What is indicated about graphic design projects?
(A) They are assigned on a weekly basis.
(B) Some are needed on a daily basis.
(C) Some are more difficult than others.
(D) They are paid a flat fee upon completion.

**185.** What will Ms. Harvey most likely do on July 14?
(A) Submit a graphic design portfolio.
(B) Travel to Palo Alto.
(C) Participate in a training session.
(D) Meet Mr. Tull.

GO ON TO THE NEXT PAGE.

| From: | Olivia Harrison <o.harrison@redstar.com> |
|---|---|
| To: | Service <bills@pacificgas.com> |
| Re: | Invoice #OHAR834-PP234 |
| Date: | June 10 |

To whom it may concern:

I am writing about my gas bill for May. You've billed me for $310.87, which is substantially higher than what I have been invoiced in previous months.

For the record, I have never been late or missed a payment, nor was I notified of a price increase, so I would like to know the reason for the sudden increase in the amount. If the amount has been billed in error, I would appreciate an adjustment to my account.

My gas meter is old and I've long wondered if it should be replaced. If a technician needs to check it, the best time would be before noon on any weekday. I prefer to be present if possible while the work is being done.

Kind regards,
Olivia Harrison

Pacific Gas
Service Technician Log Sheet—Clayton Ridge Residences
June 15

| Technician name | Address of service | Start time | Service |
|---|---|---|---|
| Samir Shah | 249 Walker Cir. | 9:22 A.M. | Meter repaired |
| Joe Petsche | 1082 Plainfield Rd. | 10:38 A.M. | Meter replaced |
| Sloane Sherwin | 1145 Cherry Tree Ln. | 1:31 P.M. | Meter replaced |
| Brandon Glover | 87 Laurel Canyon Rd. | 3:17 P.M. | Meter inspected |

| From: | Service <bills@pacificgas.com> |
|---|---|
| To: | Olivia Harrison <o.harrison@redstar.com> |
| Re: | Invoice #OHAR834-PP234 |
| Date: | June 16 |

Dear Ms. Harrison,

Thank you for contacting Pacific Gas. We have determined that a faulty meter had registered your usage incorrectly. The technician who visited your Plainfield Road residence this morning replaced the meter, and the problem should not occur again. The malfunction affects your bill for April only.

A credit in the amount of $150.70 will appear on your next bill.

If you have any question, please do not hesitate to contact us.

Sincerely,
Francine Force
Medit Power Customer Support

**186.** Why was the first e-mail sent?
(A) To sign up for online billing.
(B) To inquire about a charge.
(C) To ask for a deadline extension.
(D) To request a receipt.

**187.** What is suggested about Ms. Harrison?
(A) She has never missed a payment.
(B) She has recently moved to a different house.
(C) She has contacted Ms. Force repeatedly.
(D) She has multiple accounts with Pacific Gas.

**188.** Who visited Ms. Harrison's house on June 15?
(A) Mr. Shah.
(B) Mr. Petsche.
(C) Ms. Sherwin.
(D) Mr. Glover.

**189.** In the second e-mail, in paragraph 1, line 2 the word "usage" is closest in meaning to
(A) habit.
(B) condition.
(C) fee.
(D) amount.

**190.** What does Ms. Force indicate in her e-mail?
(A) A payment is now overdue.
(B) A new service is being offered.
(C) A new meter has been ordered.
(D) A problem was limited to one month.

GO ON TO THE NEXT PAGE.

Rocky Mountain Council for Industry & Commerce
6th Annual Solid Waste and Recycling Symposium
Parkway Plaza Casper Convention Centre
Casper, Wyoming
Saturday, April 12

Tentative Schedule

| Time | Location | |
|---|---|---|
| 9:15 A.M. - 9:45 A.M. | Welcome and Opening Remarks by RMCIC President Buck Stratham Moresche Banquet Hall | |
| | Wind River Room | Grand Teton Room |
| 10:15 A.M. - 11:45 A.M. | Beneficial Use of Drill Cuttings in Land Reclamation – J. Wallace Vicker | Creating Standards of Excellence for Safety and Quality – Devin Paul Trevino |
| 1:30 P.M. - 2:30 P.M. | A Generator's Perspective to Hazardous Materials Disposal – Sunny Stiles | Implementing Mobile Laser Scanning in Solid Waste Engineering – Tanner Cody |
| 3:15 P.M. - 4:45 P.M. | Ash Facility Management: What's In & What's Out? – Maryanne Campbell | Can Landfill Gas Cause Groundwater Contamination? – Thanasis Pashalides |

- Presenters must notify Walter Dorgan (w.dorgan@rmcic.org.) of needed changes by March 30. A final version of the schedule will be posted by April 5 on our Web site, www.rmcic.org/schedule

- Presenters MUST register for the event. Select the "Registration" tab on our Web site and fill out a registration form. Be sure to mark the box labeled, "Presenter." Additionally, those planning to **recruit** personnel should complete an Employer Application, available under the site's Career Center tab.

- The Parkway Plaza Days Inn has a limited number of rooms still available at a discounted rate, so consider booking promptly.

| From: | Maryanne Campbell <m.campbell@campbellash.com> |
|---|---|
| To: | Walter Dorgan<w.dorgan@rmcic.org> |
| Re: | Schedule change request |
| Date: | March 30 |

Dear Mr. Dorgan,

Due to circumstances beyond his control, my colleague, Thanasis Pashalides, is unable to give his presentation. I have now been asked to take over from him. Looking at the most recent draft of the conference schedule, however, I noticed that the time slot assigned to Mr. Pashalides conflicts with mine. Kindly, assist me in resolving this dilemma. Thank you.

Sincerely,
Maryanne Campbell

GO ON TO THE NEXT PAGE.

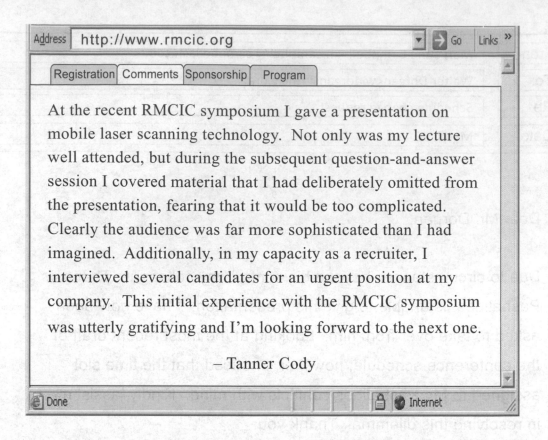

Address http://www.rmcic.org ▼ → Go Links »

| Registration | Comments | Sponsorship | Program |

At the recent RMCIC symposium I gave a presentation on mobile laser scanning technology. Not only was my lecture well attended, but during the subsequent question-and-answer session I covered material that I had deliberately omitted from the presentation, fearing that it would be too complicated. Clearly the audience was far more sophisticated than I had imagined. Additionally, in my capacity as a recruiter, I interviewed several candidates for an urgent position at my company. This initial experience with the RMCIC symposium was utterly gratifying and I'm looking forward to the next one.

– Tanner Cody

🖭 Done 🔒 🌐 Internet

**191.** What industry is the focus of the conference?
(A) Waste management.
(B) Food.
(C) Automotive.
(D) Clothing.

**192.** In the review, the word "capacity" in paragraph 1, line 5, is closest in meaning to
(A) ability.
(B) solution.
(C) role.
(D) time.

**193.** What has Ms. Campbell been asked to do?
(A) Arrange a meeting with Mr. Dorgan.
(B) Submit a draft of her presentation.
(C) Substitute for another presenter.
(D) Cancel travel arrangements made for Mr. Cody.

**194.** According to the schedule, what are presenters expected to do?
(A) Reserve hotel accommodations by April 12.
(B) Request a discount code from Parkway Plaza Days Inn.
(C) Confirm on their registration that they are presenting.
(D) Indicate where they would like their materials sent.

**195.** What is probably true about Mr. Cody?
(A) He preferred the recent RMCIC conference over previous ones.
(B) He believed his topic would be easy to understand.
(C) He recently opened an ash management company.
(D) He filled out an Employer Application when registering.

**THERMO KING COLDCASE CONTAINERS**
Mobile Refrigerated Storage Units

We provide mobile refrigeration rental units of various sizes and capacities depending on the needs of the client. Our prices are economical, and this makes our mobile refrigeration rental company much sought after by restaurants, food distributors, grocery stores, and other businesses looking for cold-storage solutions. All units include lockable door latches, non-slip flooring, and interior fluorescent light fixtures, and all are equipped with a 60-foot power cable. Our units can be delivered to any location in Texas and are available for short-term hire, monthly rental, or **annual** lease.

| Unit | Door Type | Length (feet) | Floor space (square feet) | Internal capacity (cubic feet) |
|------|-----------|---------------|---------------------------|--------------------------------|
| Economy | Single | 5 | $25ft^2$ | $125ft^3$ |
| Standard | Double | 8 | $64ft^2$ | $512ft^3$ |
| Deluxe | Double | 15 | $225ft^2$ | $3375ft^3$ |
| Deluxe Plus | Double | 20 | $400ft^2$ | $8000ft^3$ |

Whether your needs are temporary or long-term, our knowledgeable customer service representatives can recommend the ideal storage solution for you. For more information, visit http://www.thermoking.com

---

**THERMO KING COLDCASE CONTAINERS — Customer Inquiry Form**

Name: Sasha Lee

Business: Sasha's

E-mail: sasha@sashastampa.com

Date: July 22

Comments:

I heard about your company from a friend, Avi Gregorius, who rents one of your units for his business, Avi's Delicatessen. I am also a restaurant owner, and our walk-in freezer can no longer accommodate us. Thus, we require an additional Thermo King Coldcase unit that can be placed near the loading dock behind our building. We don't need a lot of extra storage space, but we do need a unit with two doors so we can easily load everything in and out. Please let me know which unit you recommend and when you can deliver it. Also, please tell me if your units contain a digital temperature display. We need to be able to closely monitor the temperature at all times. Thank you.

*GO ON TO THE NEXT PAGE.*

## Customer Review

I am very satisfied with my Thermo King Coldcase storage container, and I was quite pleased to have my first month's rental fee waived thanks to Thermo King's refer-a-friend program. I started with a smaller, 512 cubic-foot **storage** unit, but it became clear this month that I would need something one size larger. So I called Thermo King, and within a couple of hours, my sales rep, Joe Irwin, showed up with a new, larger unit. I highly recommend Thermo King Containers to all business owners for whom cold storage is a necessity.

- Sasha Lee, owner, Sasha's

---

**196.** What information about Thermo King storage units is NOT included in the advertisement?
(A) The range of temperature settings.
(B) The amount of interior space.
(C) The number of doors.
(D) The type of lighting.

**197.** What is probably true about Mr. Gregorius?
(A) He used to work with Ms. Lee.
(B) He owns a franchise.
(C) He plans to hire another butcher.
(D) He received a discount from Thermo King Containers.

**198.** What is suggested about Sasha's?
(A) Its business continues to grow.
(B) It is located near Avi's Delicatessen.
(C) It plans to extend its operating hours.
(D) Its menu features locally grown foods.

**199.** Which storage container is Ms. Lee currently using?
(A) Economy.
(B) Standard.
(C) Deluxe.
(D) Deluxe Plus.

**200.** In the review the phrase "showed up" in paragraph 1, line 5, is closest in meaning to
(A) lifted.
(B) arrived.
(C) increased.
(D) uncovered.

**Stop! This is the end of the test. If you finish before time is called, you may go back to Parts 5, 6, and 7 and check your work.**

# New TOEIC Listening Script

**PART 1**

1. (　) (A) The waiter is taking an order.
   (B) A diner is making a reservation.
   (C) A chef is pouring oil into a pan.
   (D) A manager is posting a schedule.

2. (　) (A) The man is climbing the stairs.
   (B) The man is climbing a tree.
   (C) The man is climbing down a ladder.
   (D) The man is climbing up a ladder.

3. (　) (A) The woman is exercising on the floor.
   (B) The woman is cleaning a toilet.
   (C) The woman is watching TV.
   (D) The woman is making a phone call.

4. (　) (A) The man is changing a tire.
   (B) The man is changing a battery.
   (C) The woman is changing a lightbulb.
   (D) The woman is changing her clothes.

5. (　) (A) They are in a business meeting.
   (B) They are at a sales seminar.
   (C) They are on an airplane.
   (D) They are near the ocean.

6. (　) (A) A man is waterskiing.
   (B) Some people are enjoying their food.
   (C) A girl is crying.
   (D) A woman is sewing.

*GO ON TO THE NEXT PAGE.*

# PART 2

7. (    ) Where's the best place around here to get some pizza?
       (A) I think it could have been better.
       (B) Have you tried the pizzeria on Jackson Street?
       (C) A bag of potatoes.

8. (    ) Why are so many people coming in late today?
       (A) No, the deadline is next week.
       (B) I drive to work.
       (C) The transit workers went on strike.

9. (    ) Has your phone number changed in the past year?
       (A) No, there's no entry fee.
       (B) Yes, I switched carriers last month.
       (C) I left it at home.

10. (    ) Should I make a reservation at the Japanese restaurant or the Korean one?
       (A) Either one is fine with me.
       (B) Call the restaurant for directions.
       (C) I missed my flight.

11. (    ) When do we need to be at the airport?
       (A) In Seattle.
       (B) By seven-thirty.
       (C) Several times.

12. (    ) Who will distribute the promotional materials?
       (A) No, I didn't.
       (B) Mr. Patterson will.
       (C) The address is www.openbook.com.

13. (    ) Did you see the prices on the merchandise?
       (A) I think I have room for one more.
       (B) A table for three, please.
       (C) Yes, everything is quite expensive.

14. (    ) You've met Gerald and Pam before, haven't you?
       (A) Let's meet there.
       (B) It starts tomorrow.
       (C) No, I haven't.

15. (    ) Where's the nearest post office?
        (A) It was interesting.
        (B) It leaves from platform B.
        (C) There's one across the street.

16. (    ) Would you like to join us for lunch?
        (A) That would be great.
        (B) Pasta, I think.
        (C) Yes, it's made of steel.

17. (    ) How long was Ms. Whiteside on vacation?
        (A) It's too short.
        (B) At the doctor's office.
        (C) Only for a week.

18. (    ) Why are all our desks in the hallway?
        (A) Yes, take the elevator downstairs.
        (B) On my desk is fine.
        (C) The main office is being painted.

19. (    ) What's the airfare for a non-stop flight to Miami?
        (A) At the airport.
        (B) About 500 dollars.
        (C) For six hours.

20. (    ) Are you giving your presentation this morning or in the afternoon?
        (A) Thanks for the suggestion.
        (B) A short presentation.
        (C) It's today at two.

21. (    ) Who should we send the contract to?
        (A) All parties involved.
        (B) Print it on both sides.
        (C) By express mail.

22. (    ) You are scheduled to work at the front desk on Sunday, aren't you?
        (A) Did she run there?
        (B) No, I'm off the rest of the week.
        (C) They make a good team.

*GO ON TO THE NEXT PAGE.*

23. (     ) Doesn't Sandra Park live in Phoenix?
  (A) Yes, she's been there a long time.
  (B) No, I've never tried it.
  (C) It's closed for the season.

24. (     ) Can I help you find something in your size?
  (A) There's another seating at six.
  (B) I enjoyed it very much.
  (C) That would be great.

25. (     ) When are the inventory reports due?
  (A) Because it's a large facility.
  (B) We can't afford it.
  (C) Not until the last day of October.

26. (     ) Which office are you going to request?
  (A) I haven't decided yet.
  (B) We'll see about that.
  (C) We're moving next week.

27. (     ) Do you want to discuss the project now or after the meeting?
  (A) From the project manager.
  (B) Nothing for me, thanks.
  (C) Sorry, I'm busy right now.

28. (     ) How many barrels of this wine were produced?
  (A) For the summer clearance sale.
  (B) We produced twelve hundred.
  (C) It's a great food pairing.

29. (     ) I can't get the intercom to work properly.
  (A) Here, let me help you.
  (B) Sixty-five copies.
  (C) I don't know how to get there.

30. (     ) Why don't we stop by the pub later?
  (A) Sure, if you want to.
  (B) It stops at the corner.
  (C) Yes, half an hour.

31. (　　) Don't you have the same smart phone as Annette?

    (A) Yes, but mine is the latest model.

    (B) Sometimes I do.

    (C) I always call at that time.

## PART 3

***Questions 32 through 34*** *refer to the following conversation.*

M : I'm sorry I didn't get back to you yesterday, Jessica. I've been busy planning the reception dinner for Mr. Wright. It's an important event.

W : I know. It's not often we get a visit from one of our top corporate executives. The reception is this Friday night at 7:00, right?

M : Yes, and it's being held at The Russian Tea Room, so… just a reminder. Formal wear is required.

W : Oh, no. I have to be out on a job site that afternoon. So I'll have to go home and change first. I might be a little late——is that OK?

32. (　　) What is the main topic of the conversation?

    (A) A conference presentation.

    (B) A building renovation.

    (C) A reception for an executive.

    (D) A budget review.

33. (　　) What does the man remind the woman to do?

    (A) Arrive early at an event.

    (B) Dress appropriately.

    (C) Check an account.

    (D) Reserve a table.

34. (　　) What will the woman be doing on Friday afternoon?

    (A) Working outside of the office.

    (B) Hosting an event.

    (C) Interviewing a job applicant.

    (D) Meeting a client.

***Questions 35 through 37*** *refer to the following conversation between three speakers.*

W : This is Lucy from research and development in the Granger Building. We were supposed to get a package from the Pittsburgh laboratory last week, but it never arrived.

*GO ON TO THE NEXT PAGE.*

USA M : Hang on a second. Hey, Joe! Did we receive a package from Pittsburgh? It's Lucy from R and D.

AUS M : No. I haven't seen anything.

USA M : OK, Tony says he hasn't seen anything. If you give me the tracking number, I can check our database. That will tell us if it's in the system and still in transit.

W : The tracking number is K-T-1-7-9. By the way, I was told by the technician that the package is white and has a shiny blue logo on the side. That would certainly distinguish it from the plain brown boxes we usually receive.

USA M : Thanks for that information. As soon as I find out your package's whereabouts, I'll let you know.

35. (     ) What is the purpose of the call?
      (A) To purchase some supplies.
      (B) To return some merchandise.
      (C) To make shipping arrangements.
      (D) To locate a missing item.

36. (     ) What does the American man ask for?
      (A) A tracking number.
      (B) An inventory amount.
      (C) The location of a building.
      (D) The weight of package.

37. (     ) What does the woman say about the box?
      (A) It is larger than average.
      (B) It may have been damaged.
      (C) It is needed soon.
      (D) It is not brown.

***Questions 38 through 40*** *refer to the following conversation.*

W : I'd like to reserve a table for three on the evening of April 4th, please. Are there any tables available in the first seating?

M : Yes, I have one table for three at 5:30 p.m.

W : Oh, that's too early. Is there anything a little later? I'm meeting some clients at the airport at 5:00. With traffic, there's no way we can be there by 5:30.

M : Well, I could hold the table for you until 5:45. Would that give you enough time? Otherwise, I have tables available starting at 7:30.

38. (     ) What is the woman inquiring about?
    (A) A payment option.
    (B) A ticket upgrade.
    (C) A flight schedule.
    (D) A dinner reservation.

39. (     ) What does the woman say she needs to do at 5:00 p.m.?
    (A) Give a presentation.
    (B) Rent a hotel room.
    (C) Meet some clients.
    (D) Catch a connecting flight.

40. (     ) What does the man say he can do?
    (A) Cancel a reservation.
    (B) Take a later flight.
    (C) Hold a table.
    (D) Contact a client.

**Questions 41 through 43** refer to the following conversation.

M : Hi, I see that the community recreation center offers family memberships. Are there any benefits other than pool and tennis court access?

W : Yes, the center has members-only events such as aerobics and art classes every week. Most of our events are appropriate for children and adults of all ages.

M : Count us in. Can I apply for a family membership for six people, please?

W : Sure. Please fill out this form with the names to be included in the membership and your contact information. It will take only a few minutes to print out your membership cards.

41. (     ) Where does the conversation take place?
    (A) At a library.
    (B) At a community center.
    (C) At a concert hall.
    (D) At an aquarium.

42. (     ) What additional membership benefit does the woman mention?
    (A) Special classes.
    (B) Gift certificates.
    (C) Free parking.
    (D) Discounted merchandise.

GO ON TO THE NEXT PAGE.

43. (　　) What does the woman ask the man to do?
    (A) Present photo identification.
    (B) Return at a later date.
    (C) Complete some paperwork.
    (D) Pick up a visitor's guide.

**Questions 44 through 46** _refer to the following conversation._

M : Hello, I'd like to buy this whole chicken. Is it free-range?

W : Yes, it is. In fact, these birds are particularly special. They're locally raised just down the road from here, at Daisyfield Farms.

M : That's great. I'm happy to support local farmers. These birds look so plump and juicy. I'll take two, please.

W : Certainly. Would you like some recipes? There are free cards over there that you can take if you'd like.

44. (　　) Where is the conversation most likely taking place?
    (A) At a restaurant.
    (B) At a butcher shop.
    (C) At a dry cleaners.
    (D) At a tourist center.

45. (　　) According to the woman, what is special about the product?
    (A) It is currently discounted.
    (B) It is only available today.
    (C) It is locally raised.
    (D) It is new this season.

46. (　　) What does the woman offer the man?
    (A) A business card.
    (B) An area map.
    (C) A handmade basket.
    (D) Free recipes.

**Questions 47 through 49** _refer to the following conversation._

M : Hi, Sophia. Jack Owens here. Listen, since you helped at the company's recycling drive for charity last year, I thought you might want to volunteer again this year. It's on Saturday and Sunday, the 3rd and 4th of next month.

W : I'd be glad to help out. I'm free Saturday afternoon.

M : That's what I was afraid of. I'm way over-staffed on Saturday afternoon. But we're desperate for people on Sunday morning. Are you available at any time that day?

W : Sorry, I can't do it on Sunday. I wish I could help out, but I think you'll have to find someone else this time.

47. (     ) Why is the man calling?
    (A) To recruit staff for an event.
    (B) To find a substitute for a night shift.
    (C) To ask for donations.
    (D) To cancel an advertisement.

48. (     ) What does the man mean when he says, "That's what I was afraid of"?
    (A) He expected the woman's response.
    (B) He didn't understand the woman's response.
    (C) He feared the woman's reaction.
    (D) He didn't appreciate the woman's reaction.

49. (     ) What will the man have to do?
    (A) Create a job description.
    (B) Reschedule a training session.
    (C) Try to find another volunteer.
    (D) Work the shift himself.

**Questions 50 through 52** refer to the following conversation.

M : Hello, Ms. Biggs, this is Luke Ledesma, the building superintendent. We'll be doing routine maintenance in your apartment later this week——just servicing the ventilation systems, checking the smoke detectors, and such. And I'd like to find out when is the best time for us to come.

W : Actually, I'm leaving for vacation tomorrow. And I won't be back till next Sunday evening, so I won't be here when you're doing the maintenance.

M : That's not a problem. I can let the workers into your apartment. The only thing I'll need you to do before you leave is move your furniture away from the vents, so they'll be easier to get to.

50. (     ) Why is the man calling?
    (A) To offer a new product.
    (B) To follow up on an estimate.
    (C) To inquire about a lease.
    (D) To arrange a maintenance visit.

*GO ON TO THE NEXT PAGE.*

51. (    ) What does the woman say she will be doing tomorrow?
        (A) Looking at apartments.
        (B) Attending a workshop.
        (C) Going on a trip.
        (D) Hosting a party.

52. (    ) What does the man ask the woman to do?
        (A) Make a deposit.
        (B) Complete a survey.
        (C) Move some furniture.
        (D) Leave a key at the front desk.

**Questions 53 through 55** *refer to the following conversation.*

W : Thanks for coming to see me, Steve.  As you know, Baker and Associates is expanding and we'd like to start offering an online version of our popular technology magazine.  My management team would like you to lead the project.  Would you be interested?

M : Wow, I'd love to.  But I have to wonder, why me?  There are plenty of people on the staff who've worked on the tech magazine much longer than I have.

W : Yes, but your extensive website management experience is a game-changer.  We think this would be especially useful for launching an online magazine.  We're confident that you'll produce an outstanding product.

53. (    ) According to the woman, what is the company planning to do?
        (A) Merge with a media company.
        (B) Start an online magazine.
        (C) Relocate its headquarters.
        (D) Sponsor a local sports team.

54. (    ) What does the woman ask the man to do?
        (A) Meet with a client.
        (B) Lead a project.
        (C) Train some employees.
        (D) Write an article.

55. (    ) Why has the management chosen the man?
        (A) He is a professional cyclist.
        (B) He has lived abroad.
        (C) He has experience in Web site management.
        (D) He has organized many corporate events.

W : Hi, this is Judy Sheen, the tenant of apartment 8B at Stratford Place. I wanted to let your office know that I'm going to be moving out at the end of the month. I've been transferred to my company's headquarters in Los Angeles.

M : Well, I hope that's good news for you, but as stated in a lease agreement, we require one month notice before you move out. So you'll still be responsible for the next month's rent.

W : Would it be possible to waive that portion of the rent? I'll be happy to find someone to sublet the apartment when I leave.

56. (       ) Why is the woman moving?
  (A) Her lease has been expired.
  (B) She is being transferred to a different city.
  (C) There has been an increase in the rent.
  (D) The apartment offers no parking.

57. (       ) What does the woman ask the man to do?
  (A) Contact the moving company.
  (B) Help her move out.
  (C) Reduce a payment.
  (D) Store some of her belongings.

58. (       ) What does the woman offer to do?
  (A) Find a new tenant.
  (B) Call the real estate agent.
  (C) Write out a check.
  (D) Sign the lease.

*Questions 59 through 61* *refer to the following conversation.*

W : Hey, Rex. The driver who usually delivers our merchandise to Carver's Department Store called in sick this morning. Do you think you can make his two o'clock delivery for him this afternoon?

M : Sure, no problem, but I've never made any deliveries to McCormick's, so I'll need some directions. How do I get there from our warehouse?

W : I suggest taking Interstate 90 to North Lake Shore Drive. You can't miss it. Once you're there, don't forget to have the shipping supervisor sign the delivery confirmation form.

*GO ON TO THE NEXT PAGE.*

59. (　　) What does the woman ask the man to do?
    (A) Work overtime.
    (B) Prepare an invoice.
    (C) Schedule an appointment.
    (D) Make a coworker's delivery.

60. (　　) What does the man say he needs?
    (A) Keys to a vehicle.
    (B) A telephone number.
    (C) A price list.
    (D) Directions to a location.

61. (　　) What does the woman remind the man to do?
    (A) Print a document.
    (B) Get a signature.
    (C) Keep his receipts.
    (D) Check some merchandise.

**_Questions 62 through 64_** _refer to the following conversation and invoice._

W : Will that be all for today?  Just a new phone and service upgrade?

M : I do have one more question before I buy the phone.  Can I pay my bill online?  I travel a lot for work and I'm not at home when the bills come.

W : Absolutely.  You can set up a payment account on our website.  I also recommend downloading a mobile phone application so you can view the status of your account anytime.

M : OK, great.  But I changed my mind about the extended warranty.  I don't think I really need it.  Could you remove that from my bill?

W : Of course.

62. (　　) Who is the woman?
    (A) A store clerk.
    (B) A real estate agent.
    (C) A banker.
    (D) A teacher.

63. (　　) What does the man ask about?
    (A) Additional features.
    (B) Online payments.
    (C) Trade-in policies.
    (D) Coverage area.

64. (    ) Look at the graphic.  Which charge will be removed from the bill?
   - (A) $75.00.
   - (B) $76.56.
   - (C) $100.
   - (D) $700.

| Description | Unit Price | Total |
|---|---|---|
| FZR 9980 Silver 16GB GSM | $700.00 | $700.00 |
| Two-year Extended Warranty | $100.00 | $100.00 |
| Diamond Unlimited Service Plan (monthly) | $75.00 | $75.00 |
| Subtotal | | $875.00 |
| Sales Tax | | $76.56 |
| Shipping & Handling | | $0.00 |
| Total Due | | $951.56 |

Due upon receipt

Thank you for your business!

**Questions 65 through 67** refer to the following conversation and notice.

W : Ray, there's a new concert series opening at the Royal Oak Theater and some of us from work are planning to go.  Are you interested?

M : Sure, I've read about the series.  Sounds like there's going to be a lot of great music.  How much are tickets?

W : It depends.  Look, here's the information.  We already have more than ten people committed to attending, so we should qualify for that price.

M : That's certainly reasonable.  Would that be for this weekend?

W : Yes, after work on Friday.

M : Is someone going to order the tickets in advance?

W : Lou in the marketing department is.  You could give him a call and let him know to include you.

65. (    ) What type of event are the speakers discussing?
   - (A) A theater performance.
   - (B) A museum exhibit opening.
   - (C) A photography workshop.
   - (D) A live music concert.

GO ON TO THE NEXT PAGE.

66. (      ) Look at the graphic.  What ticket price will the speakers probably pay?
   (A) $15.
   (B) $18.
   (C) $20.
   (D) $25.

| Admission Price per Person | |
| --- | --- |
| University student | $18 |
| Group of 10 or more | $20 |
| Member | $15 |
| Nonmember | $25 |

67. (      ) What does the woman suggest the man do?
   (A) Pay with a credit card.
   (B) Rent some equipment.
   (C) Leave work early.
   (D) Call a coworker.

*Questions 68 through 70* refer to the following conversation and e-mail.

M : Hey, Joyce, are you able to access the Internet from your workstation?

W : Yeah.  I haven't had any issues with it lately, Eric.  Actually, my connection has been a little bit faster than usual.

M : Well, I can't even connect to it, so I can't read my email.  Did anything from Beau with the latest sales report come yet?

W : Just a few minutes ago.  Do you want me to send a reply?

M : That won't be necessary but could you print it out for me?  I need a copy of the sales report for the meeting this afternoon.

68. (      ) Why is the man unable to access his e-mail?
   (A) His password has expired.
   (B) His Internet connection is not working.
   (C) He forgot to update some software.
   (D) He cancelled his Internet subscription.

69. (    ) Look at the graphic. Who sent the e-mail the speakers are referring to?

    (A) Beau Tremonte.

    (B) Eric Plonkenberg.

    (C) Vivian Wu.

    (D) Joyce Figg.

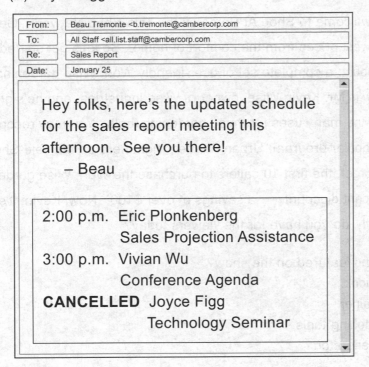

| From: | Beau Tremonte <b.tremonte@cambercorp.com |
| To: | All Staff <all.list.staff@cambercorp.com |
| Re: | Sales Report |
| Date: | January 25 |

Hey folks, here's the updated schedule for the sales report meeting this afternoon. See you there!
   – Beau

2:00 p.m.  Eric Plonkenberg
             Sales Projection Assistance

3:00 p.m.  Vivian Wu
             Conference Agenda

**CANCELLED**  Joyce Figg
             Technology Seminar

70. (    ) What does the man ask the woman to do?

    (A) Print out a document.

    (B) Review some sales figures.

    (C) Inspect his computer.

    (D) Prepare some training materials.

GO ON TO THE NEXT PAGE.

### PART 4

Questions 71 through 73 *refer to the following broadcast.*

I'm Athena Vargos and welcome to Shop At Home on the Tele-Shop Network. Get the latest products at the lowest prices from the comfort of home. So let's get started with this week's featured product: a complete set of user-friendly Work Wise gardening tools. Here with me now is Mr. Kevin Wise, owner of Wise Industries, and he's going to demonstrate some of the many uses for these gardening tools. You may recognize him as the host of the popular program "Urban Farmer," right here on the Tele-Shop Network. But before I forget, the first 10 callers to purchase the Work Wise gardening set will receive a 25 percent discount——a savings of over $100! Now, Kevin, it's good to see you. What, exactly, do you have for the viewers today?

71. (　　) What item is being featured on the show?
    (A) A self-help book.
    (B) A plant container.
    (C) A set of gardening tools.
    (D) A portable generator.

72. (　　) What is Mr. Wise going to do?
    (A) Demonstrate the use of a product.
    (B) Answer questions from viewers.
    (C) Introduce the next guest.
    (D) Show a short video.

73. (　　) What is offered to the first 10 callers?
    (A) A ticket to the show.
    (B) Free shipping on an order.
    (C) A club membership.
    (D) A significant discount.

Questions 74 through 76 *refer to the following telephone message.*

Hi, Fiona. It's Richard. Look, I know it's your day-off, but we've got a couple of problems here this morning. We're almost ready to open, but I'm getting worried. Topper's Bakery hasn't delivered our pastries, and Charles hasn't arrived with our dairy order, and we're always his first stop of the morning. I've tried calling but I can't get through to either of them. Don't forget, we have that order of 30 scones and coffee for

Handley Trading at 8:15. Meanwhile, we have enough milk for maybe an hour of the morning rush. After that, we're in big trouble. It's 5:57, and I'm about to open the doors. Please call me back and let me know what to do.

74. (    ) Where, most likely, does the speaker work?
    (A) At a convenience store.
    (B) At a talent agency.
    (C) At a brokerage firm.
    (D) At a cafe.

75. (    ) What is the problem?
    (A) Some items have not been delivered.
    (B) Some money is missing.
    (C) Some files have been misplaced..
    (D) Some customers are waiting.

76. (    ) What does the speaker mean by, "We're in big trouble"?
    (A) They will open an hour later.
    (B) They will fail an inspection.
    (C) They will be out of dairy products.
    (D) They will fire some employees.

**Questions 77 through 79** *refer to the following talk.*

Would everybody please take their seats? OK… I'd like begin this training session for fleet operators of our new Clyster X300 diesel forklifts. You'll notice an attendance sheet is being passed around. Don't forget to include your employee number, so you'll be credited for attending this training. Your 8-digit number is on the back of your company identification card, by the way. After we covered the traffic safety rules of the warehouse floor, I'll walk you through the main forklift routes. When this part of the training session is over, you'll meet our driving instructors who will guide you through your first hands-on experience with the new equipment. Let's get started.

77. (    ) What is the speaker about to do?
    (A) Issue identification cards.
    (B) Create work teams.
    (C) Talk about safety guidelines.
    (D) Inspect some equipment.

*GO ON TO THE NEXT PAGE.*

78. (      ) What are the listeners asked to provide?
  (A) An employee number.
  (B) A driver's license.
  (C) A personal reference.
  (D) An e-mail address.

79. (      ) What will happen at the end of the session?
  (A) A user's manual will be distributed.
  (B) Operators will use the new equipment.
  (C) A supervisor will hand out forms.
  (D) Participants will ask questions.

**_Questions 80 through 82 refer to the following telephone message._**

Hey, Vicki. It's Carl Rogers. We're so lucky you've decided to join us on the logistics committee for this summer's branding conference in Orlando. I just e-mailed you a list of hotels near the conference center. Could you go through the list and contact the hotels underlined about whether or not they can accommodate our team? So far we have 12 associates confirmed for the trip, so we'll need at least 14 rooms. That number could go as high as 20. We'll see. Also, please inquire about meeting facilities at each hotel. We'll want to meet every morning before heading over to the conference. OK. Let me know what you find out and we'll take it from there. I'm at extension 13.

80. (      ) What has the listener agreed to do?
  (A) Prepare some training materials.
  (B) Deliver some packages.
  (C) Speak at an event.
  (D) Help plan a conference.

81. (      ) What did the speaker send in an e-mail?
  (A) A registration form.
  (B) A tentative itinerary.
  (C) A list of hotels.
  (D) A flight schedule.

82. (      ) What is the speaker specifically interested in?
  (A) Price per room.
  (B) Transportation.
  (C) Internet access.
  (D) Meeting facilities.

I'm pleased to officially announce that our merger with Meridian Savings and Trust is now complete. Beginning January 1, our two banks will become Meridian Sterling Bank. We expect this merger to have a substantial and positive impact on you as our employees. First of all, as most of you know, we're relocating to Centennial Tower, located in the heart of downtown, with multiple bus and subway lines. It's going to be much easier on those of you who commute from the suburbs. Additionally, we will integrate many of Meridian's employment policies; for instance, vacation and paid leave. So, all employees will now have three extra days of vacation per calendar year. Sounds pretty good so far, doesn't it?

83. (      ) What kind of business does the speaker work in?
 (A) Banking.
 (B) Travel.
 (C) Retail sales.
 (D) Auto insurance.

84. (      ) According to the speaker, what advantage does the new location have?
 (A) It has more parking spaces.
 (B) It uses green technology.
 (C) It is easily accessible by public transportation.
 (D) It is close to a variety of restaurants.

85. (      ) What policy change does the speaker mention?
 (A) Weekly meetings will be optional.
 (B) Travel expenses will be reimbursed.
 (C) Employees will have more vacation time.
 (D) Telecommuting options will be offered.

*Questions 86 through 88* refer to the following recorded message.

This is an automated message to all Kast Construction Company employees. Due to severe weather conditions predicted for Tuesday evening, our Tampa office will be closed tomorrow, Wednesday, July 17. Local weather reports indicate that Hurricane Tina will bring winds of 85 mph after weakening from its Category 2 status Tuesday morning. Despite the weakening, Tina still poses a significant threat to the peninsula.

GO ON TO THE NEXT PAGE.

As a precaution, we're asking all Tampa staff to shut down and completely unplug all electronic devices such as computers and printers. Barring any unforeseen circumstances, the Tampa office will reopen Thursday, July 18. Thank you.

86. (     ) What is the main purpose of the message?
    (A) To announce a closing.
    (B) To request a deadline extension.
    (C) To report a network issue.
    (D) To explain a firing decision.

87. (     ) What is expected to happen by the evening?
    (A) New security measures will go into effect.
    (B) Weather conditions will be severe.
    (C) Power will be restored.
    (D) Construction will begin.

88. (     ) What are listeners reminded to do?
    (A) Update a schedule.
    (B) Locate a contractor.
    (C) Report damage to a supervisor.
    (D) Turn off some equipment.

*Questions 89 through 91* *refer to the following excerpt from a meeting.*

Thank you very much, Mr. Franklin. I would like to add my own hello and welcome to everyone and to thank all the members for your wonderful reception when I joined the board in August. To cut to the chase, you've seen our latest budget report. Business has steadily decreased in spite of our efforts to attract guests. //Adding insult to injury, there are plans to build a new hotel across the street.// It's an understatement to say that drastic measures are in order. Now, I'm sure many of you are hesitant to spend a lot of money on renovations, but let's face it; our facilities are outdated and our image is in dire need of a facelift.

89. (     ) Who are the listeners?
    (A) Engineers.
    (B) Beauticians.
    (C) Board members.
    (D) News reporters.

90. (     ) What does the speaker mean when he says "Adding insult to injury"?
   (A) To emphasize the point.
   (B) To lessen our burden.
   (C) To make a long story short.
   (D) To make things worse.

91. (     ) What does the speaker propose?
   (A) Launching an advertising campaign.
   (B) Lodging a formal complaint.
   (C) Renovating a facility.
   (D) Merging with a competitor.

**Questions 92 through 94** *refer to the following announcement and advertisement.*

Attention, Tiger Mart shoppers. This month, Tiger Mart is celebrating its 21st anniversary. In celebration, we'll be having a massive two-for-one blow-out sale in each of our four locations. Here at our store, buy one Wearlite 30-gallon storage box and get the second one free! But please check our advertisement, since each store location has two-for-one deals on different items. And for even more savings, visit our website to become a member of our Tiger Mart Rewards Program. There you'll find all the information you need to sign up and start saving.

92. (     ) Look at the graphic. At which store location is the announcement being made?
   (A) Hinsdale.
   (B) Downers Grove.
   (C) Woodridge.
   (D) Burr Ridge.

| Tiger Mart Anniversary Two-for-One Blow Out Sale! | |
| --- | --- |
| **Sales Item** | **Store Location** |
| Storage Boxes | Woodridge |
| Water purification filters | Willowbrook |
| Car wax and polish | Downers Grove |
| Desk lamps | Burr Ridge |

*GO ON TO THE NEXT PAGE.*

93. (     ) What is Tiger Mart celebrating?
    (A) A national holiday.
    (B) A profitable quarter.
    (C) An anniversary.
    (D) A new store opening.

94. (     ) Why should listeners visit a Web site?
    (A) To check for coupons.
    (B) To write a customer review.
    (C) To vote for the employee of the week.
    (D) To sign up for a rewards program.

**Questions 95 through 97** *refer to the following telephone message and floor plan.*

Hi, Oliver, it's Michelle.  I know I asked you to drop off the employee progress reports by the end of today, but I just remembered that I'm going to be at the Baltimore office all day tomorrow.  So just go ahead and leave it on my desk whenever you have a chance, and I'll review the reports when I return on Friday.  Oh, I just moved to a new office on the sixth floor.  To get here, exit the elevator and start heading toward the lobby.  Make a right after you pass the reception desk and walk straight.  When you reach the bathroom, take another right and I'm the first door on your left.

95. (     ) What type of report is the speaker requesting?
    (A) Office inventory.
    (B) Employee evaluations.
    (C) Expense reports.
    (D) Travel receipts.

96. (     )  Look at the graphic.  Which office belongs to the speaker?
    (A) Office 1.
    (B) Office 2.
    (C) Office 3.
    (D) Office 4.

97. (　　) Why does the speaker postpone a deadline?
        (A) She wants a job to be done thoroughly.
        (B) She needs to interview more people.
        (C) She knows the listener is busy.
        (D) She will not be able to review some documents until later.

**Questions 98 through 100** *refer to the following talk and schedule.*

Good morning and welcome back to Day 2 of our cross-training program. Before we begin today's assignment in the personnel department, I'd like to point out a change on the schedule. We will be working in the technical support center on Thursday morning. However, Friday morning will now be spent in the warehouse. And remember that this training program includes lunch. Today's meal will be catered by the Italian restaurant across the street. We'll break for lunch around 11:45, and then head up to purchasing around 1:30.

98. (　　) When is this talk most likely taking place?
        (A) On Monday.
        (B) On Tuesday.
        (C) On Thursday.
        (D) On Friday.

99. (　　) Look at the graphic. Which department will listeners visit on Friday afternoon?
        (A) Technical support.
        (B) Purchasing.
        (C) Marketing.
        (D) Personnel.

### CROSS-TRAINING SCHEDULE

| Department | / | Date |
|---|---|---|
| Personnel | / | Monday (a.m.) – Tuesday (a.m.) |
| Purchasing | / | Monday (p.m.) – Tuesday (p.m.) |
| Warehouse | / | Wednesday |
| Technical support | / | Thursday (a.m.) – Friday (a.m.) |
| Marketing | / | Thursday (p.m.) – Friday (p.m.) |

100. (　　) What will happen after the morning session?
        (A) Instructors will give a demonstration.
        (B) A meeting will be held.
        (C) Identification cards will be distributed.
        (D) Lunch will be provided.

*GO ON TO THE NEXT PAGE.*

**NO TEST MATERIAL ON THIS PAGE**

# New TOEIC Speaking Test

## Question 1: Read a Text Aloud

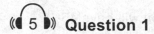 **Question 1**

**Directions:** In this part of the test, you will read aloud the text on the screen. You will have 45 seconds to prepare. Then you will have 45 seconds to read the text aloud.

Those who think education has little bearing on success throw out the names of famous university dropouts like Bill Gates and Steve Jobs while proponents of a college degree quote statistic after statistic to prove its impact on a person's employability and earnings. People with experience but no formal degree could be favored for certain jobs, but they may struggle to advance professionally. On the other hand, a college grad with the best education and book smarts may be completely at sea when it comes to dealing with real-world work situations with no prior industry experience, and struggle to land that first job.

| PREPARATION TIME |
|:---:|
| 00 : 00 : 45 |

| RESPONSE TIME |
|:---:|
| 00 : 00 : 45 |

*GO ON TO THE NEXT PAGE.*

# Question 2: Read a Text Aloud

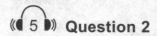 **Question 2**

**Directions:** In this part of the test, you will read aloud the text on the screen. You will have 45 seconds to prepare. Then you will have 45 seconds to read the text aloud.

Japan is building the world's fastest supercomputer, which it hopes will make the country the new global hub for artificial intelligence research. The supercomputer is expected to run at a speed of 130 petaflops, meaning it is able to perform a mind-boggling 130 quadrillion calculations per second (that's 130 million billion). Once complete, the AI Bridging Cloud Infrastructure (ABCI) will be the most powerful supercomputer in the world, surpassing the current champion, China's Sunway TaihuLight, currently operating at 93 petaflops.

| PREPARATION TIME |
| :---: |
| 00 : 00 : 45 |

| RESPONSE TIME |
| :---: |
| 00 : 00 : 45 |

# Question 3: Describe a Picture

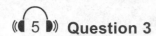 **Question 3**

**Directions:** In this part of the test, you will describe the picture on your screen in as much detail as you can.  You will have 30 seconds to prepare your response.  Then you will have 45 seconds to speak about the picture.

PREPARATION TIME

00 : 00 : 30

RESPONSE TIME

00 : 00 : 45

*GO ON TO THE NEXT PAGE.*

# Question 3: Describe a Picture

## 答題範例

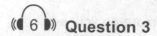 **Question 3**

Some people are posing for a picture.

They appear to be having a party.

They appear to be in a nightclub.

All but one person in the picture is wearing sunglasses.

Four people are holding champagne glasses.

They are all well-dressed.

There is glitter and confetti in the air.

The woman on the left is wearing a party hat.

The guy in the middle has his arms out and palms facing upward.

They are most likely celebrating a special occasion.

If I had to guess, I'd say it's New Year's Eve.

They look abnormally happy, but it is a party after all.

The people are all smiling or have happy expressions.

Before the picture was taken, they were probably dancing.

It is impossible to say for sure but it looks like their champagne

  glasses are empty.

The people are glamorous and attractive.

The women appear to be looking toward the ceiling.

The man second from the right is the tallest of the group.

# Questions 4-6: Respond to Questions

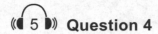 **Question 4**

**Directions:** In this part of the test, you will answer three questions. For each question, begin responding immediately after you hear a beep. No preparation time is provided. You will have 15 seconds to respond to Questions 4 and 5 and 30 seconds to respond to Question 6.

Imagine that you are participating in a research study about your sleeping habits. You have agreed to answer some questions in a telephone interview.

## Question 4
Do you get the recommended 7 to 8 hours of sleep per night?

## Question 5
Do you feel that the amount of sleep you get is enough for your lifestyle?

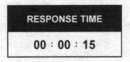

## Question 6
How would you rate the quality of your sleep? Do you sleep soundly at night?

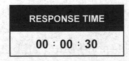

*GO ON TO THE NEXT PAGE.*

# Questions 4-6: Respond to Questions

## 答題範例

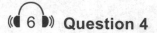 **Question 4**

Do you get the recommended 7 to 8 hours of sleep per night?

**Answer**

> Yes, I generally do.
>
> There are exceptions of course.
>
> If I don't get enough sleep, I make up for it on the weekend.

 **Question 5**

Do you feel that the amount of sleep you get is enough for your lifestyle?

**Answer**

> Yes, I think I get the right amount of sleep.
>
> I'm busy, but not too busy to get enough rest.
>
> I have an active lifestyle but it all balances out.

# Questions 4-6: Respond to Questions

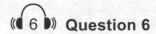 **Question 6**

How would you rate the quality of your sleep? Do you sleep soundly at night?

## Answer

On a scale of 1 to 10, I'd rate the quality of my sleep to

be about an 8.

Occasionally, I will have a hard time falling asleep.

It's usually because I'm excited about something that will

happen the next day.


Once I fall asleep, I'm out like a light.

I have to set two different alarms to make sure I wake up

on time in the morning.

It's sometimes difficult to wake me.


Overall, the quality of my sleep is very satisfactory.

If I'm feeling particularly tired, I'll make sure to take a nap

or go to bed early.

I'm much more productive when I'm well-rested.

*GO ON TO THE NEXT PAGE.*

# Questions 7-9: Respond to Questions Using Information Provided

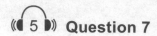 **Question 7**

**Directions:** In this part of the test, you will answer three questions based on the information provided. You will have 30 seconds to read the information before the questions begin. For each question, begin responding immediately after you hear a beep. No additional preparation time is provided. You will have 15 seconds to respond to Questions 7 and 8 and 30 seconds to respond to Question 9.

Riverside Food Co-Op
*Announcing our new Farm Share Program*

Riverside Food Co-Op in Riverside, California, invites you to participate in its community-supported Farm Share program. Members enjoy fresh farm produce during our growing season from April to November.

**Register for Farm Share and receive these benefits:**
- Lifetime membership in the Riverside Food Co-Op, giving you direct access to local growers and vendors
- More than 25 varieties of in-season vegetables, fruits, and herbs, harvested by local producers and delivered fresh to your home by our staff
- A selection of pick-your-own citrus fruits, bananas and avocados, and other fruits
- Access to our member Web site with Food Co-Op updates and a Farm Share newsletter
- Discounts on events at the Co-Op for the annual summer music festival. Events cost $15, but members pay $10.

Members receive a farm share once a week. A full-size share is $675, and a half-size share is $350. Half-size shareholders receive half of the full-sized share of produce each week. Our farm produce is locally-grown without the use of pesticides and herbicides. All producers are Certified Organic. For more information or to sign up for a share, please visit our Web site, www.riversidefood.org

> Hi! This is Randy Morris. I'm calling about the food co-op. Would you mind if I asked a few questions?

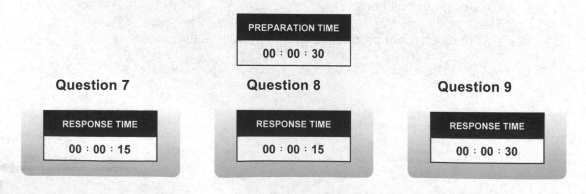

# Questions 7-9: Respond to Questions Using Information Provided

## 答題範例

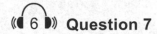 **Question 7**

When does the Farm Share program take place?

**Answer**

> The Farm Share program is active from April to November.
>
> This is related to the growing season.
>
> We do not operate during the winter months.

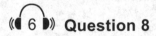 **Question 8**

How often do Farm Share shipments arrive and how much are they?

**Answer**

> Once a week for the duration of the program.
>
> A full-size share is $675, and a half-size share is $350.
>
> Half-size shareholders receive half of the full-sized share
>
> of produce each week.

*GO ON TO THE NEXT PAGE.*

# Questions 7-9: Respond to Questions Using Information Provided

What are some of the benefits of the Farm Share program?

## Answer

One benefit is membership in the Riverside Food Co-Op, giving you direct access to local growers and vendors. You can choose between more than 25 varieties of in-season vegetables, fruits, and herbs, harvested by local producers and delivered fresh to your home by our staff. We also have a selection of pick-your-own citrus fruits, bananas and avocados, and other fruits.

You'll get access to our member Web site with Food Co-Op updates. You'll receive a Farm Share newsletter. You'll also be eligible for discounts on events at the Co-Op for the annual summer music festival.

# Question 10: Propose a Solution

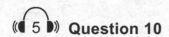 **Question 10**

**Directions:** In this part of the test, you will be presented with a problem and
asked to propose a solution. You will have 30 seconds to
prepare. Then you will have 60 seconds to speak. In your
response, be sure to show that you recognize the problem, and
propose a way of dealing with the problem.

In your response, be sure to

- show that you recognize the caller's problem, and
- propose a way of dealing with the problem.

| PREPARATION TIME |
|---|
| 00 : 00 : 30 |

| RESPONSE TIME |
|---|
| 00 : 01 : 00 |

*GO ON TO THE NEXT PAGE.*

# Question 10: Propose a Solution

## 答題範例

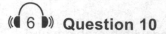 **Question 10**

**Voice Message**

Hello. This is Mick Sweeney. Two days ago, I ordered three books on your website with the next-day delivery, which guaranteed my books would be delivered to my house by the following day. I paid extra for the special delivery because I wanted those books before I leave the country in two days. As stated on your website, if the order is placed before 1 p.m., you should have received the order on the same day and have shipped the books by yesterday at the latest. Today is already Friday, and I haven't received my books yet. Please let me know what happened. You can contact me on my cell phone at (313) 566-7890.

# Question 10: Propose a Solution

## 答題範例

**Hello Mr. Sweeney.**

This is Jerry Thomas calling you from Booksworld.com.

I am calling regarding your voice message.

You placed an order for three books from our website two days ago with next-day delivery.

This means you were supposed to receive your books the next day on Thursday.

Unfortunately, you haven't received your package yet.

First of all, I am very sorry for the delivery problem.

I looked up your order record and details, and I don't know why you did not receive your order the next day.

There must have been some confusion in the delivery system.

It is not very common at all for us to have complaints about our deliveries.

**Anyway, I placed the same order with next-day delivery so you can have the books by tomorrow.**

That way, you'll have them before you leave the country.

And you will also get a refund of the $10 delivery charge as Booksworld.com credit.

Once again, I apologize for the inconvenience.

If you have any further questions, you can reach me at (313) 340-0500.

Meanwhile, I'd like to ask a favor.

Would you please give me a call once you've received the books?

I'd like to confirm the delivery.

Thank you.

*GO ON TO THE NEXT PAGE.*

# Question 11: Express an Opinion

 **Question 11**

**Directions:** In this part of the test, you will give your opinion about a specific topic. Be sure to say as much as you can in the time allowed. You will have 15 seconds to prepare. Then you will have 60 seconds to speak.

If you could study a subject that you have never had the opportunity to study, what would you choose? Explain your choice, using specific reasons and details.

| PREPARATION TIME |
| :---: |
| 00 : 00 : 15 |

| RESPONSE TIME |
| :---: |
| 00 : 01 : 00 |

# Question 11: Express an Opinion

## 答題範例

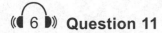 **Question 11**

I've always wanted to study architecture.

Ever since I was child, I've enjoyed drawing buildings.

At one point, I even drafted a few floor plans.

Architecture is a creative and artful way to make an impact on society.

After all, architects build modern structures to fit the needs of the world.

They help shape a city through the creation of functional buildings.

Each architectural piece is a creative representation of the thoughts and hopes of the designer.

Of course, it's important to meet the needs and expectations of your clients.

But the overall look, design and feel of your work is generally a result of your own creativity.

Tourists travel great distances in search of famous pieces of architecture.

The Great Pyramid of Giza, Big Ben, the Golden Gate Bridge, and the Taj Mahal are just a few world-renowned structures.

Even if I didn't ultimately create the next Eiffel Tower or Empire State Building, my works would generally be outside, meaning that they would be seen by the public.

Architecture demands attention to detail and focused work.

It is not a data-entry job.

It takes long hours and expertise to create a masterpiece and earn the commission that comes along with it.

If I studied architecture, I would concentrate on larger structures.

I would like to design a museum, or maybe even a hotel.

I think I'd make a good architect.

*GO ON TO THE NEXT PAGE.*

**NO TEST MATERIAL ON THIS PAGE**

# New TOEIC Writing Test

## Questions 1-5: Write a Sentence Based on a Picture

### Question 1

**Directions:** Write ONE sentence based on the picture using the TWO words or phrases under it. You may change the forms of the words and you may use them in any order.

**push / street**

GO ON TO THE NEXT PAGE

# Questions 1-5: Write a Sentence Based on a Picture

## Question 2

**Directions:** Write ONE sentence based on the picture using the TWO words or phrases under it. You may change the forms of the words and you may use them in any order.

**group / under**

# Questions 1-5: Write a Sentence Based on a Picture

## Question 3

**Directions:** Write ONE sentence based on the picture using the TWO words or phrases under it. You may change the forms of the words and you may use them in any order.

**judge / gavel**

*GO ON TO THE NEXT PAGE*

# Questions 1-5: Write a Sentence Based on a Picture

## Question 4

**Directions:** Write ONE sentence based on the picture using the TWO words or phrases under it. You may change the forms of the words and you may use them in any order.

**water / garden**

# Questions 1-5: Write a Sentence Based on a Picture

## Question 5

**Directions:** Write ONE sentence based on the picture using the TWO words
or phrases under it. You may change the forms of the words and
you may use them in any order.

**collision / head on**

GO ON TO THE NEXT PAGE.

# Questions 6-7: Respond to a written request

## Question 6

**Directions:** Read the e-mail below.

| |
|---|
| **From:** Rick Moss <r_moss@tmail.com> |
| **To:** Kyle Patrick <deltarunners@yahoo.com> |
| **Subject:** Running Club |
| **Sent:** Sunday, October 12 |

Hello Kyle,

I found your group online while searching for running clubs in Atlanta. Any chance you're still taking members? I'm a fairly experienced distance runner, and I'm planning to train for the upcoming Atlanta Marathon. If you are accepting members, could you give me some information about the club?

I look forward to hearing from you.

Thanks in advance,
Rick Moss

**Directions:** Write Rick as the leader of the running group. Invite him to join the group and give at least (2) two details about the group, i.e. when and where it meets, etc.

# Questions 6-7: Respond to a written request

## 答題範例

## Question 6

Rick,

Thanks for inquiring about the Delta Running Club. As it happens, we just had a spot open up and I'd like to invite you to join us. We meet every morning except Sundays in front of the public library on Winslow Avenue in Atlanta. Our group runs normally cover 10k, and we usually separate into sub-groups depending upon levels of endurance, speed, age, etc. Our routes are always posted a week in advance on the Web site, and we encourage club members to suggest new routes. So don't be shy!

As for the size of the group, we've put a cap on 50 people; 50 being the most manageable and productive size, but the actual number of runners who show up every day will vary. However, we are seeking dedicated runners who are either, like yourself, training for an event, or willing to commit to a certain number of days per week.

Let me know if you decide to accept this invitation.

Yours,
Kyle Patrick
President, Delta Running Club

GO ON TO THE NEXT PAGE.

# Questions 6-7: Respond to a written request

## Question 7

Directions: Read the e-mail below.

| |
|---|
| From:  Lowell George |
| Sent:  Saturday, May 17 |
| To:  Leslie Brown |
| Subject:  Laundry room issues |

Leslie,

As your tenant relations manager, I am tasked with reminding you about our standard rules of etiquette practiced in our laundry facilities.  I have recently received a number of complaints from residents who have reported their clothes being removed from the dryer and left to sit damp and wrinkled on the counter.  The offender is then using the dryer for their own clothing.  This is not only rude, but technically criminal, since the dryers aren't free.  It's stealing, basically.

While I do not wish to improperly accuse you of any wrongdoing, several residents have pointed the finger at you.  Whether or not this is true, I can't say for sure.  However, I am compelled to remind you that under no circumstances are residents permitted to touch the personal belongings of others.  This is true even if someone has left their clothing in a dryer and the time has expired.

Furthermore, I am now forced to install a security camera in the laundry room in hopes of ceasing this activity.  Again, I'm not accusing you of anything.  I'm simply reminding you of the rules.  If you have any questions, please contact me ASAP.

Yours,
Lowell

Directions:  You're upset about the accusation and haven't used the laundry room in six months.  Explain why.

# Questions 6-7: Respond to a written request

## 答題範例

## Question 7

Hi Lowell,

First of all, I'm offended by the accusations. That certain residents would point the finger at me for such boorish behavior is not surprising, given my relationship with some of them. I have a good idea who it is, though. As you well know, not everybody in the building gets along.

Anyway, the fact is I haven't used the laundry room in over six months; since I took a new job across town, I'm sending all my laundry to a cleaning service. In fact, you can check the delivery logs at the front desk. Honeybee Cleaners. They pick-up on Tuesday and deliver on Wednesday. So, I definitely couldn't be the person responsible, and frankly, would never stoop to such petty behavior.

Sincerely,

Leslie

GO ON TO THE NEXT PAGE

# Questions 8: Write an opinion essay

## Question 8

**Directions:** Read the question below.  You have 30 minutes to plan, write, and revise your essay.  Typically, an effective response will contain a minimum of 300 words.

If you could ask a historical figure from the past one question, what would you ask?  Why?  Use specific reasons and details to support your answer.

# Questions 8: Write an opinion essay

## 答題範例

## Question 8

My question would be for Adolph Hitler, and it would appear to be a very simple question, but it is actually quite complicated. The question would be why? What happened in your life that led you to believe that a certain group of people, the Jews, deserved to be exterminated? And what gave you the right to think that you should be the one to carry out this genocide? I don't have any questions about how you carried out the Holocaust——that's been explained by the history books. I want to know what happened to you personally that made you hate Jews and try to kill all of them? Not just the ones that did you harm. All of them.

I want to know because I find it utterly incomprehensible for one human being to have such violent antipathy toward his fellowman. After all, no matter who we are, we're all the same flesh and blood. I can't conceive of wanting to kill a single person, let alone an entire ethnic group. Surely, even if there were a few bad Jews, how could you overlook their contributions to society as a whole. Jews have done many, many great things for humanity. Certainly, they weren't starting wars or trying to take over Germany. Thus, I think something happened to you early in life. Maybe you were ashamed of the fact that you had Jewish heritage in your family lineage. That's right. You were part Jewish. So, something terrible happened to you, and I want to know what it was. I think everybody in the world should know so we don't let it happen to some other kid who may grow up to wipe out a different group of people.

Mostly, I would want to ask this question because it's a very human question. It goes right to the heart of your conflict. I'm awfully sorry you had to live the life you did, but I'm even more sorry for the millions of lives you so senselessly destroyed.

# TOEIC ANSWER SHEET

REGISTRATION No.

姓 名
N A M E

## READING SECTION

### Part 5

| No. | ANSWER A B C D | No. | ANSWER A B C D | No. | ANSWER A B C D |
|---|---|---|---|---|---|
| 101 | Ⓐ Ⓑ Ⓒ Ⓓ | 111 | Ⓐ Ⓑ Ⓒ Ⓓ | 121 | Ⓐ Ⓑ Ⓒ Ⓓ |
| 102 | Ⓐ Ⓑ Ⓒ Ⓓ | 112 | Ⓐ Ⓑ Ⓒ Ⓓ | 122 | Ⓐ Ⓑ Ⓒ Ⓓ |
| 103 | Ⓐ Ⓑ Ⓒ Ⓓ | 113 | Ⓐ Ⓑ Ⓒ Ⓓ | 123 | Ⓐ Ⓑ Ⓒ Ⓓ |
| 104 | Ⓐ Ⓑ Ⓒ Ⓓ | 114 | Ⓐ Ⓑ Ⓒ Ⓓ | 124 | Ⓐ Ⓑ Ⓒ Ⓓ |
| 105 | Ⓐ Ⓑ Ⓒ Ⓓ | 115 | Ⓐ Ⓑ Ⓒ Ⓓ | 125 | Ⓐ Ⓑ Ⓒ Ⓓ |
| 106 | Ⓐ Ⓑ Ⓒ Ⓓ | 116 | Ⓐ Ⓑ Ⓒ Ⓓ | 126 | Ⓐ Ⓑ Ⓒ Ⓓ |
| 107 | Ⓐ Ⓑ Ⓒ Ⓓ | 117 | Ⓐ Ⓑ Ⓒ Ⓓ | 127 | Ⓐ Ⓑ Ⓒ Ⓓ |
| 108 | Ⓐ Ⓑ Ⓒ Ⓓ | 118 | Ⓐ Ⓑ Ⓒ Ⓓ | 128 | Ⓐ Ⓑ Ⓒ Ⓓ |
| 109 | Ⓐ Ⓑ Ⓒ Ⓓ | 119 | Ⓐ Ⓑ Ⓒ Ⓓ | 129 | Ⓐ Ⓑ Ⓒ Ⓓ |
| 110 | Ⓐ Ⓑ Ⓒ Ⓓ | 120 | Ⓐ Ⓑ Ⓒ Ⓓ | 130 | Ⓐ Ⓑ Ⓒ Ⓓ |

### Part 6

| No. | ANSWER A B C D | No. | ANSWER A B C D |
|---|---|---|---|
| 131 | Ⓐ Ⓑ Ⓒ Ⓓ | 141 | Ⓐ Ⓑ Ⓒ Ⓓ |
| 132 | Ⓐ Ⓑ Ⓒ Ⓓ | 142 | Ⓐ Ⓑ Ⓒ Ⓓ |
| 133 | Ⓐ Ⓑ Ⓒ Ⓓ | 143 | Ⓐ Ⓑ Ⓒ Ⓓ |
| 134 | Ⓐ Ⓑ Ⓒ Ⓓ | 144 | Ⓐ Ⓑ Ⓒ Ⓓ |
| 135 | Ⓐ Ⓑ Ⓒ Ⓓ | 145 | Ⓐ Ⓑ Ⓒ Ⓓ |
| 136 | Ⓐ Ⓑ Ⓒ Ⓓ | 146 | Ⓐ Ⓑ Ⓒ Ⓓ |
| 137 | Ⓐ Ⓑ Ⓒ Ⓓ | 147 | Ⓐ Ⓑ Ⓒ Ⓓ |
| 138 | Ⓐ Ⓑ Ⓒ Ⓓ | 148 | Ⓐ Ⓑ Ⓒ Ⓓ |
| 139 | Ⓐ Ⓑ Ⓒ Ⓓ | 149 | Ⓐ Ⓑ Ⓒ Ⓓ |
| 140 | Ⓐ Ⓑ Ⓒ Ⓓ | 150 | Ⓐ Ⓑ Ⓒ Ⓓ |

### Part 7

| No. | ANSWER A B C D | No. | ANSWER A B C D | No. | ANSWER A B C D | No. | ANSWER A B C D | No. | ANSWER A B C D |
|---|---|---|---|---|---|---|---|---|---|
| 151 | Ⓐ Ⓑ Ⓒ Ⓓ | 161 | Ⓐ Ⓑ Ⓒ Ⓓ | 171 | Ⓐ Ⓑ Ⓒ Ⓓ | 181 | Ⓐ Ⓑ Ⓒ Ⓓ | 191 | Ⓐ Ⓑ Ⓒ Ⓓ |
| 152 | Ⓐ Ⓑ Ⓒ Ⓓ | 162 | Ⓐ Ⓑ Ⓒ Ⓓ | 172 | Ⓐ Ⓑ Ⓒ Ⓓ | 182 | Ⓐ Ⓑ Ⓒ Ⓓ | 192 | Ⓐ Ⓑ Ⓒ Ⓓ |
| 153 | Ⓐ Ⓑ Ⓒ Ⓓ | 163 | Ⓐ Ⓑ Ⓒ Ⓓ | 173 | Ⓐ Ⓑ Ⓒ Ⓓ | 183 | Ⓐ Ⓑ Ⓒ Ⓓ | 193 | Ⓐ Ⓑ Ⓒ Ⓓ |
| 154 | Ⓐ Ⓑ Ⓒ Ⓓ | 164 | Ⓐ Ⓑ Ⓒ Ⓓ | 174 | Ⓐ Ⓑ Ⓒ Ⓓ | 184 | Ⓐ Ⓑ Ⓒ Ⓓ | 194 | Ⓐ Ⓑ Ⓒ Ⓓ |
| 155 | Ⓐ Ⓑ Ⓒ Ⓓ | 165 | Ⓐ Ⓑ Ⓒ Ⓓ | 175 | Ⓐ Ⓑ Ⓒ Ⓓ | 185 | Ⓐ Ⓑ Ⓒ Ⓓ | 195 | Ⓐ Ⓑ Ⓒ Ⓓ |
| 156 | Ⓐ Ⓑ Ⓒ Ⓓ | 166 | Ⓐ Ⓑ Ⓒ Ⓓ | 176 | Ⓐ Ⓑ Ⓒ Ⓓ | 186 | Ⓐ Ⓑ Ⓒ Ⓓ | 196 | Ⓐ Ⓑ Ⓒ Ⓓ |
| 157 | Ⓐ Ⓑ Ⓒ Ⓓ | 167 | Ⓐ Ⓑ Ⓒ Ⓓ | 177 | Ⓐ Ⓑ Ⓒ Ⓓ | 187 | Ⓐ Ⓑ Ⓒ Ⓓ | 197 | Ⓐ Ⓑ Ⓒ Ⓓ |
| 158 | Ⓐ Ⓑ Ⓒ Ⓓ | 168 | Ⓐ Ⓑ Ⓒ Ⓓ | 178 | Ⓐ Ⓑ Ⓒ Ⓓ | 188 | Ⓐ Ⓑ Ⓒ Ⓓ | 198 | Ⓐ Ⓑ Ⓒ Ⓓ |
| 159 | Ⓐ Ⓑ Ⓒ Ⓓ | 169 | Ⓐ Ⓑ Ⓒ Ⓓ | 179 | Ⓐ Ⓑ Ⓒ Ⓓ | 189 | Ⓐ Ⓑ Ⓒ Ⓓ | 199 | Ⓐ Ⓑ Ⓒ Ⓓ |
| 160 | Ⓐ Ⓑ Ⓒ Ⓓ | 170 | Ⓐ Ⓑ Ⓒ Ⓓ | 180 | Ⓐ Ⓑ Ⓒ Ⓓ | 190 | Ⓐ Ⓑ Ⓒ Ⓓ | 200 | Ⓐ Ⓑ Ⓒ Ⓓ |

## LISTENING SECTION

### Part 1

| No. | ANSWER A B C D |
|---|---|
| 1 | Ⓐ Ⓑ Ⓒ Ⓓ |
| 2 | Ⓐ Ⓑ Ⓒ Ⓓ |
| 3 | Ⓐ Ⓑ Ⓒ Ⓓ |
| 4 | Ⓐ Ⓑ Ⓒ Ⓓ |
| 5 | Ⓐ Ⓑ Ⓒ Ⓓ |
| 6 | Ⓐ Ⓑ Ⓒ Ⓓ |
| 7 | Ⓐ Ⓑ Ⓒ |
| 8 | Ⓐ Ⓑ Ⓒ |
| 9 | Ⓐ Ⓑ Ⓒ |
| 10 | Ⓐ Ⓑ Ⓒ |

### Part 2

| No. | ANSWER A B C D | No. | ANSWER A B C D |
|---|---|---|---|
| 11 | Ⓐ Ⓑ Ⓒ | 21 | Ⓐ Ⓑ Ⓒ |
| 12 | Ⓐ Ⓑ Ⓒ | 22 | Ⓐ Ⓑ Ⓒ |
| 13 | Ⓐ Ⓑ Ⓒ | 23 | Ⓐ Ⓑ Ⓒ |
| 14 | Ⓐ Ⓑ Ⓒ | 24 | Ⓐ Ⓑ Ⓒ |
| 15 | Ⓐ Ⓑ Ⓒ | 25 | Ⓐ Ⓑ Ⓒ |
| 16 | Ⓐ Ⓑ Ⓒ | 26 | Ⓐ Ⓑ Ⓒ |
| 17 | Ⓐ Ⓑ Ⓒ | 27 | Ⓐ Ⓑ Ⓒ |
| 18 | Ⓐ Ⓑ Ⓒ | 28 | Ⓐ Ⓑ Ⓒ |
| 19 | Ⓐ Ⓑ Ⓒ | 29 | Ⓐ Ⓑ Ⓒ |
| 20 | Ⓐ Ⓑ Ⓒ | 30 | Ⓐ Ⓑ Ⓒ |

| No. | ANSWER A B C D |
|---|---|
| 31 | Ⓐ Ⓑ Ⓒ |
| 32 | Ⓐ Ⓑ Ⓒ |
| 33 | Ⓐ Ⓑ Ⓒ Ⓓ |
| 34 | Ⓐ Ⓑ Ⓒ Ⓓ |
| 35 | Ⓐ Ⓑ Ⓒ Ⓓ |
| 36 | Ⓐ Ⓑ Ⓒ Ⓓ |
| 37 | Ⓐ Ⓑ Ⓒ Ⓓ |
| 38 | Ⓐ Ⓑ Ⓒ Ⓓ |
| 39 | Ⓐ Ⓑ Ⓒ Ⓓ |
| 40 | Ⓐ Ⓑ Ⓒ Ⓓ |

### Part 3

| No. | ANSWER A B C D | No. | ANSWER A B C D |
|---|---|---|---|
| 41 | Ⓐ Ⓑ Ⓒ Ⓓ | 51 | Ⓐ Ⓑ Ⓒ Ⓓ |
| 42 | Ⓐ Ⓑ Ⓒ Ⓓ | 52 | Ⓐ Ⓑ Ⓒ Ⓓ |
| 43 | Ⓐ Ⓑ Ⓒ Ⓓ | 53 | Ⓐ Ⓑ Ⓒ Ⓓ |
| 44 | Ⓐ Ⓑ Ⓒ Ⓓ | 54 | Ⓐ Ⓑ Ⓒ Ⓓ |
| 45 | Ⓐ Ⓑ Ⓒ Ⓓ | 55 | Ⓐ Ⓑ Ⓒ Ⓓ |
| 46 | Ⓐ Ⓑ Ⓒ Ⓓ | 56 | Ⓐ Ⓑ Ⓒ Ⓓ |
| 47 | Ⓐ Ⓑ Ⓒ Ⓓ | 57 | Ⓐ Ⓑ Ⓒ Ⓓ |
| 48 | Ⓐ Ⓑ Ⓒ Ⓓ | 58 | Ⓐ Ⓑ Ⓒ Ⓓ |
| 49 | Ⓐ Ⓑ Ⓒ Ⓓ | 59 | Ⓐ Ⓑ Ⓒ Ⓓ |
| 50 | Ⓐ Ⓑ Ⓒ Ⓓ | 60 | Ⓐ Ⓑ Ⓒ Ⓓ |

| No. | ANSWER A B C D |
|---|---|
| 61 | Ⓐ Ⓑ Ⓒ Ⓓ |
| 62 | Ⓐ Ⓑ Ⓒ Ⓓ |
| 63 | Ⓐ Ⓑ Ⓒ Ⓓ |
| 64 | Ⓐ Ⓑ Ⓒ Ⓓ |
| 65 | Ⓐ Ⓑ Ⓒ Ⓓ |
| 66 | Ⓐ Ⓑ Ⓒ Ⓓ |
| 67 | Ⓐ Ⓑ Ⓒ Ⓓ |
| 68 | Ⓐ Ⓑ Ⓒ Ⓓ |
| 69 | Ⓐ Ⓑ Ⓒ Ⓓ |
| 70 | Ⓐ Ⓑ Ⓒ Ⓓ |

### Part 4

| No. | ANSWER A B C D | No. | ANSWER A B C D |
|---|---|---|---|
| 71 | Ⓐ Ⓑ Ⓒ Ⓓ | 81 | Ⓐ Ⓑ Ⓒ Ⓓ |
| 72 | Ⓐ Ⓑ Ⓒ Ⓓ | 82 | Ⓐ Ⓑ Ⓒ Ⓓ |
| 73 | Ⓐ Ⓑ Ⓒ Ⓓ | 83 | Ⓐ Ⓑ Ⓒ Ⓓ |
| 74 | Ⓐ Ⓑ Ⓒ Ⓓ | 84 | Ⓐ Ⓑ Ⓒ Ⓓ |
| 75 | Ⓐ Ⓑ Ⓒ Ⓓ | 85 | Ⓐ Ⓑ Ⓒ Ⓓ |
| 76 | Ⓐ Ⓑ Ⓒ Ⓓ | 86 | Ⓐ Ⓑ Ⓒ Ⓓ |
| 77 | Ⓐ Ⓑ Ⓒ Ⓓ | 87 | Ⓐ Ⓑ Ⓒ Ⓓ |
| 78 | Ⓐ Ⓑ Ⓒ Ⓓ | 88 | Ⓐ Ⓑ Ⓒ Ⓓ |
| 79 | Ⓐ Ⓑ Ⓒ Ⓓ | 89 | Ⓐ Ⓑ Ⓒ Ⓓ |
| 80 | Ⓐ Ⓑ Ⓒ Ⓓ | 90 | Ⓐ Ⓑ Ⓒ Ⓓ |

| No. | ANSWER A B C D |
|---|---|
| 91 | Ⓐ Ⓑ Ⓒ Ⓓ |
| 92 | Ⓐ Ⓑ Ⓒ Ⓓ |
| 93 | Ⓐ Ⓑ Ⓒ Ⓓ |
| 94 | Ⓐ Ⓑ Ⓒ Ⓓ |
| 95 | Ⓐ Ⓑ Ⓒ Ⓓ |
| 96 | Ⓐ Ⓑ Ⓒ Ⓓ |
| 97 | Ⓐ Ⓑ Ⓒ Ⓓ |
| 98 | Ⓐ Ⓑ Ⓒ Ⓓ |
| 99 | Ⓐ Ⓑ Ⓒ Ⓓ |
| 100 | Ⓐ Ⓑ Ⓒ Ⓓ |